3rd Degree

Also by James Patterson

The Thomas Berryman Number
Season of the Machete
See How They Run
The Midnight Club
Along Came a Spider
Kiss the Girls
Hide & Seek
Jack & Jill
Miracle on the 17th Green
  (with Peter de Jonge)
Cat & Mouse
When the Wind Blows
Pop Goes the Weasel
Black Friday
Cradle and All
Roses Are Red
1st to Die
Suzanne's Diary for Nicholas
Violets Are Blue
2nd Chance (with Andrew Gross)
The Beach House (with Peter de Jonge)
Four Blind Mice
The Jester (with Andrew Gross)
The Lake House
The Big Bad Wolf

3rd Degree

A NOVEL BY

James Patterson

AND

Andrew Gross

Doubleday Large Print Home Library Edition

LITTLE, BROWN AND COMPANY

NEW YORK   BOSTON

This Large Print Edition, prepared especially for Doubleday Large Print Home Library, contains the complete, unabridged text of the original Publisher's Edition.

Little, Brown and Company
Time Warner Book Group
1271 Avenue of the Americas, New York, NY 10020

The characters and events in this book are fictitious. Any similarity to real persons, living or dead, is coincidental and not intended by the author.

ISBN 0-7394-4043-8

Printed in the United States of America

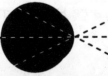

**This Large Print Book carries the
Seal of Approval of N.A.V.H.**

As always, our grateful thanks and appreciation to Homicide Inspector Holly Pera and her partner, Joe Toomey, of the San Francisco PD for handling this stuff day to day, which we only write about. And for introducing us to Dino Zografos of the Special Weapons and Tactics Group, who made the dread of a ticking bomb something real and manageable. And to Sergeant Joe Sanchez and (ret.) Inspector Steve Engler of the Berkeley Police Department, who were there during the craziness of the sixties and who brought The People's Republic of Berkeley back alive for us for a few hours, in its devastation and its dream.

And for Chuck Zion, a rare breed if there ever was one, who died in the World Trade Center, September 11, 2001.

Part One

Chapter 1

It was a clear, calm, lazy April morning, the day the worst week of my life began.

I was jogging down by the bay with my border collie, Martha. It's my thing Sunday mornings—get up early and cram my meaningful other into the front seat of the Explorer. I try to huff out three miles, from Fort Mason down to the bridge and back. Just enough to convince myself I'm bordering on something called *in shape* at thirty-six.

That morning, my buddy Jill came along. To give her baby Lab, Otis, a run, or so she claimed. More likely, to warm herself up for a bike sprint up Mount Tamalpais or whatever Jill would do for *real* exercise later in the day.

It was hard to believe that it had been only five months since Jill lost her baby. Now here she was, her body toned and lean again.

"So, how did it go last night?" she asked, shuffling sideways beside me. "Word on the street is, Lindsay had a date."

"You could call it a date . . . ," I said, focusing on the heights of Fort Mason, which weren't getting closer fast enough for me. "You could call Baghdad a vacation spot, too."

She winced. "Sorry I brought it up."

All run long, my head had been filled with the annoying recollection of Franklin Fratelli, "asset remarketing" mogul (which was a fancy way of saying he sent goons after the dot-com busts who could no longer make the payments on their Beemers and Franck Mullers). For two months Fratelli had stuck his face in my office every time he was in the Hall, until he wore me down enough to ask him up for a meal on Saturday night (the short ribs braised in port wine I had to pack back into the fridge after he bailed on me at the last minute).

"I got stood up," I said, mid-stride. "Don't ask, I won't tell the details."

We pulled up at the end of Marina Green, a lung-clearing bray from me while Mary Decker over there bobbed on her toes as if she could go another loop.

"I don't know how you do it," I said, hands on hips, trying to catch my breath.

"My grandmother," she said, shrugging and stretching out a hamstring. "She started walking five miles a day when she was sixty. She's ninety now. We have no idea where she is."

We both started to laugh. It was good to see the old Jill trying to peek through. It was good to hear the laughter back in her voice.

"You up for a mochachino?" I asked. "Martha's buying."

"Can't. Steve's flying in from Chicago. He wants to bike up to see the Dean Friedlich exhibit at the Legion of Honor as soon as he can get in and change. You know what the puppy's like when he doesn't get his exercise."

I frowned. "Somehow it's hard for me to think of Steve as a puppy."

Jill nodded and pulled off her sweatshirt, lifting her arms.

"Jill," I gasped, "what the hell is *that?*"

Peeking out through the strap of her exercise bra were a couple of small, dark bruises, like finger marks.

She tossed her sweatshirt over her shoulder, seemingly caught off guard. "Mashed myself getting out of the shower," she said. "You should get a load of how *it* looks." She winked.

I nodded, but something about the bruise didn't sit well with me. "You sure you don't want that coffee?" I asked.

"Sorry . . . You know El Exigente, if I'm five minutes late, he starts to see it as a pattern." She whistled for Otis and began to jog back to her car. She waved. "See you at work."

"So how about you?" I knelt down to Martha. "You look like a mochachino would do the trick." I snapped on her leash and started to trot off toward the Starbucks on Chestnut.

The Marina has always been one of my favorite neighborhoods. Curling streets of colorful, restored town houses. Families, the sound of gulls, the sea air off the bay.

I crossed Alhambra, my eye drifting to a beautiful three-story town house I always passed and admired. Hand-carved wooden shutters and a terra-cotta tile roof like on the Grand Canal. I held Martha as a car passed by.

That's what I remembered about the moment. The neighborhood just waking up. A redheaded kid in a FUBU sweatshirt practicing tricks on his Razor. A woman in overalls hurrying around the corner, carrying a bundle of clothes.

"C'mon, Martha." I tugged on her leash. "I can taste that mochachino."

Then the town house with the terra-cotta roof exploded into flames. I mean, it was as if San Francisco were suddenly Beirut.

Chapter 2

"Oh, my God!" I gasped as a flash of heat and debris nearly knocked me to the ground.

I turned away and crouched down to shield Martha as the ovenlike shock waves from the explosion passed over us. A few seconds later, I turned to pull myself up. Mother of God . . . I couldn't believe my eyes. The town house I had just admired was now a shell. Fire ripped through the second floor.

In that instant I realized that people could still be inside.

I tied Martha to a lamppost. Flames gusted just fifty feet away. I ran across the street to the blazing home. The second floor was gone. Anyone up there didn't have a chance.

I fumbled through my fanny pack for the cell phone. Frantically, I punched in 911. "This is Lieutenant Lindsay Boxer, San Francisco Police Department, Shield two-seven-two-one. There's been an explosion at the corner of Alhambra and Pierce. A residence. Casualties likely. Need full medical and fire support. Get them moving!"

I cut off the dispatcher. Procedure told me to wait, but if anyone was in there, there was no time. I ripped off my sweatshirt and wrapped it loosely around my face. "Oh, Jesus Christ, Lindsay," I said, and held my breath.

Then I pushed my way into the burning house.

"Is anyone there?" I shouted, choking immediately on the gray, raspy smoke. The intense heat bit at my eyes and face, and it hurt just to peek out from the protective cloth. A wall of burning Sheetrock and plaster hung above me.

"Police!" I shouted again. "Is anyone there?"

The smoke felt like sharp razors slicing into my lungs. It was impossible to hear above the roar of the flames. I suddenly understood how people trapped in fires on high floors would leap to their death rather than bear the intolerable heat.

I shielded my eyes, pushing my way through the billowing smoke. I hollered a last time, "Is anyone alive in here?"

I couldn't go any farther. My eyebrows were singed. I realized I could die in there.

I turned and headed for the light and cool that I knew were behind me. Suddenly, I spotted two shapes, the bodies of a woman and a man. Clearly dead, their clothes on fire.

I stopped, feeling my stomach turn. But there was nothing I could do for them.

Then I heard a muffled noise. I didn't know if it was real. I stopped, tried to listen above the rumble of the fire. I could hardly bear the pain of the blistering heat on my face.

There it was again. It was real, all right.

Someone was crying.

Chapter 3

I gulped air and headed deeper into the collapsing house. "Where are you?" I called. I stumbled over flaming rubble. I was scared now, not only for whoever had cried but for myself.

I heard it again. A low whimpering from somewhere in the back of the house. I made straight for it. "I'm coming!" I shouted. To my left, a wooden beam crashed. The farther I went, the more trouble I was in. I spotted a hallway where I thought the sounds came from, the ceiling teetering where the second story used to be.

"Police!" I yelled. "Where are you?"

Nothing.

Then I heard the crying again. Closer this time. I stumbled down the hallway, blanketing my face. *C'mon, Lindsay . . . Just a few more feet.*

I pushed through a smoking doorway. *Jesus, it's a kid's bedroom.* What was left of it.

A bed was overturned on its side up against a wall. It was smothered in thick dust. I shouted, then heard the noise again. A muffled, coughing sound.

The frame of the bed was hot to the touch, but I managed to budge it a little bit from the wall. *Oh, my God . . .* I saw the shadowy outline of a child's face.

It was a small boy. Maybe ten years old.

The child was coughing and crying. He could barely speak. His room was buried under an avalanche of debris. I couldn't wait. Any longer and the fumes alone would kill us.

"I'm gonna get you out of here," I promised. Then I wedged myself between the wall and the bed and, with all my strength, pried it away from the wall. I took the boy by the shoulders, praying I wasn't doing him harm.

I stumbled through the flames, carrying

the boy. Smoke was everywhere, searing and noxious. I saw a light where I thought I had come in, but I didn't know for sure.

I was coughing, the boy clinging to me with his petrified grip. "Mommy, mommy," he was crying. I squeezed him back, to let him know I wasn't going to let him die.

I screamed ahead, praying that someone would answer. "Please, is anyone there?"

"Here," I heard a voice through the blackness.

I stumbled over debris, avoiding new hot spots flaming up. Now I saw the entrance. Sirens, voices. The shape of a man. A fireman. He gently took the boy out of my arms. Another fireman wrapped his arms around me. We headed outside.

Then I was out, dropping to my knees, sucking in mouthfuls of precious air. An EMT carefully put a blanket around me. Everyone was being so good, so professional. I collapsed against a fire truck up on the sidewalk. I almost threw up, then I did.

Someone put an oxygen mask over my mouth and I took several deep gulps. A fireman bent over me. "Were you inside when it went?"

"No." I shook my head. "I went in to help." I could barely talk, or think. I opened my fanny pack and showed him my badge. "Lieutenant Boxer," I said, coughing. "Homicide."

Chapter 4

"I'm all right," I said, forcing myself out of the EMT's grasp. I made my way over to the boy, who was already strapped onto a gurney. He was being wheeled into a van. The only motion in his face was a slight flickering in his eyes. But he was alive. My God, I had saved his life.

Out on the street, onlookers were being ringed back by the police. I saw the red-headed kid who'd been riding his Razor. Other horrified faces crowded around.

All of a sudden I became aware of barking. Jesus, it was Martha, still tied to the post. I ran over to her and hugged her tightly as she licked my face.

A fireman made his way to me, a division captain's crest on his helmet. "I'm Captain Ed Noroski. You okay?"

"I think so," I said, not sure.

"You guys in the Hall can't be heroes enough on your own shift, Lieutenant?" Captain Noroski said.

"I was jogging by. I saw it blow. Looked like a gas explosion. I just did what I thought was right."

"Well, you did good, Lieutenant." The fire captain looked at the wreckage. "But this was no gas explosion."

"I saw two bodies inside."

"Yeah," Noroski said, nodding. "Man and a woman. Another adult in a back room on the first floor. That kid's lucky you got him out."

"Yeah," I said. My chest was filling with dread. If this was no gas explosion . . .

Then I spotted Warren Jacobi, my number one inspector, coming out of the crowd, badging his way over to me. Warren had the "front nine," what we call the Sunday morning shift when the weather gets warm.

Jacobi had a paunchy ham hock of a face that never seemed to smile even when he told a joke, and deep, hooded eyes impossible to light up with surprise. But when he fixed on the hole where 210 Alhambra used to be and saw *me,* sooty, smeared, sitting down, trying to catch my breath — Jacobi did a double take.

"Lieutenant? You okay?"

"I think so." I tried to pull myself up.

He looked at the house, then at me again. "Seems a bit run-down, even for your normal fixer-upper, Lieutenant. I'm sure you'll do wonders with it." He held in his grin. "We have a Palestinian delegation in town I know nothing about?"

I told him what I had seen. No smoke or fire, the second floor suddenly blowing out.

"My twenty-seven years on the job gives me the premonition we're not talking busted boiler here," said Jacobi.

"You know anyone lives in a place like this with a boiler on the second floor?"

"No one I know lives in a place like this. You sure you don't want to go to the hospital?" Jacobi bent down over me. Ever since I'd taken a shot in the Coombs case, Jacobi'd become like a protective uncle with me. He had even cut down on his stupid sexist jokes.

"No, Warren, I'm all right."

I don't even know what made me notice it. It was just sitting there on the sidewalk, leaning up against a parked car, and I thought, *Shit, Lindsay, that shouldn't be there.*

Not with everything that had just gone on.

A red school knapsack. A million students carry them. Just sitting there.

I started to panic again.

I'd heard of secondary explosions in the Middle East. If it was a bomb that had gone off in the house, who the hell knew? My eyes went wide. My gaze was fixed on the red bag.

I grabbed Jacobi. "Warren, I want everyone moved back away from here, *now*. Move everybody back, now!"

Chapter 5

From the back of a basement closet, Claire Washburn pulled out an old, familiar case she hadn't seen in years. "Oh, my God . . ."

She had woken up early that morning, and after a cup of coffee on the deck, hearing the jays back for the first time that season, she threw on a denim shirt and jeans and set out on the dreaded task of cleaning out the basement closet.

First to go were the stacks of old board games they hadn't played in years. Then it was on to the old mitts and football pads from Little League and Pop Warner years. A quilt folded up that was now just a dust convention.

Then she came upon the old aluminum case buried under a musty blanket. *My God.*

Her old cello. Claire smiled at the memory. Good Lord, it had been ten years since she'd held it in her hands.

She yanked it from the bottom of the closet. Just seeing it brought back a swell of memories: hours and hours of learning the scales, practicing. "A house without music," her mother used to say, "is a house without life." Her husband Edmund's fortieth birthday, when she had struggled through the first movement of Haydn's Concerto in D— the last time she had played.

Claire unsnapped the clips and stared at the wood grain on the cello. It was still beautiful, a scholarship gift from the music department at Hampton. Before she realized she would never be a Yo-Yo Ma and headed to med school, it had been her most cherished possession.

A melody popped into her head. That same, difficult passage that had always eluded her. The first movement of Haydn's Concerto in D. Claire looked around, as if embarrassed. What the hell, Edmund was still sleeping. No one would hear.

Claire lifted her cello out of the felt mold. She took out the bow, held it in her hands. *Wow . . .*

A long minute of tuning, the old strings stretching back into their accustomed notes. A single pass, just running the bow along the strings, brought back a zillion sensations. Goose bumps. She played the first bars of the concerto. Sounded a little off, but the feel came back to her. "Ha, the old girl's still got it," she said with a laugh. She closed her eyes and played a little more.

Then she noticed Edmund, still in his pajamas, watching her, standing at the bottom of the stairs. "I know I'm out of bed"—he scratched his head—"I remember putting on my glasses, even brushing my teeth. But it can't be, 'cause I must be dreaming."

Edmund hummed the opening bars that Claire had just played. "So, you think you can finish off the next passage? That's the tricky part."

"Is that a dare, Maestro Washburn?"

Edmund smiled mischievously.

It was then that the phone rang. Edmund

picked up a cordless on the handset. "Saved by the bell," he groaned. "It's the office. On Sunday, Claire. Can't they *ever* give you a break?"

Claire took the phone. It was Freddie Rodriguez, a staffer at the ME's office. Claire listened, then she set down the phone.

"My God, Edmund . . . there's been an explosion downtown! Lindsay's been hurt."

CHAPTER 6

I don't know what took hold of me. Maybe it was the thought of the three dead people in the house, or all the cops and firemen charging around the accident scene. I stared at that knapsack, and my brain was shouting out that it was wrong—dead wrong. "Everyone get back!" I yelled again.

I started toward the knapsack. I didn't know what I was going to do yet, but the area had to be cleared.

"No way, LT." Jacobi reached for my arm. "You don't get to do this, Lindsay."

I pulled away from him. "Get everyone out of here, Warren."

"I may not outrank you, LT," Jacobi said, more impassioned this time, "but I've got fourteen more years on the force. I'm telling you, don't go near that bag."

The fire captain rushed up, shouting into his handheld, "Possible explosive device. Move everybody back. Get Magitakos from the Bomb Squad up here."

Less than a minute later, Niko Magitakos, head of the city's bomb squad, and two professionals covered in heavy protective gear pushed past me, heading toward the red bag. Niko wheeled out a boxlike instrument, an X-ray scanner. A square armored truck, like a huge refrigerator, backed up ominously toward the spot.

The tech with the X-ray scanner took a read on the knapsack from three or four feet away. I was sure the bag was hot—or at least a leave-behind. I was praying, *Don't let this blow*.

"Get the truck in here." Niko turned with a frown. "It looks hot."

In the next minutes, reinforced steel curtains were pulled out of the truck and set up in a protective barrier. A tech wheeled in a claw and crept closer to the bag. If it was a bomb, it could go off any second.

I found myself in no-man's-land, not wanting to move. A bead of sweat trickled down my cheek.

The man with the claw lifted the backpack to transport it to the truck.

Nothing happened.

"I don't get any reading," the tech holding the electrosensor said. "We're gonna go for a hand entry."

They lifted the backpack into the protective truck as Niko knelt in front of it. With practiced hands, he opened the zippered back.

"There's no charge," Niko said. "It's a fucking battery radio."

There was a collective sigh. I pulled out of the crowd and ran to the bag. There was an ID tag on the strap, one of those plastic labels. I lifted the strap and read.

BOOM! FUCKERS.

I was right. It was a goddamn leave-behind. Inside the backpack, next to the standard clock radio, was a photo in a frame. A computer photo, printed on paper, from a digital camera. The face of a good-looking man, maybe forty.

One of the charred bodies inside, I was pretty sure.

MORTON LIGHTOWER, read the inscription, AN ENEMY OF THE PEOPLE.

"LET THE VOICE OF THE PEOPLE BE HEARD."

A name was printed at the bottom. AUGUST SPIES.

Jesus, this was an execution!

My stomach turned.

Chapter 7

We got the town house ID'd pretty quickly. It did belong to the guy in the picture, Morton Lightower, and his family. The name rang a bell with Jacobi. "Isn't that the guy who owned that X/L Systems?"

"No idea." I shook my head.

"You know. The Internet honcho. Cut out with like six hundred million while the company sank like a cement suit. Stock used to sell for sixty bucks, now it's something like sixty cents."

Suddenly I remembered seeing it on the news. "The Creed of Greed guy." He was trying to buy ball teams, gobbling up lavish homes, installing a $50,000 security gate on his place in Aspen, at the same time he was dumping his own stock and laying off half his staff.

"I've heard of investor backlash," Jacobi said, shaking his head, "but this is a little much."

Behind me, I heard a woman yelling to let her through the crowd. Inspector Paul Chin ushered her forward, through the web of news vans and camera crews. She stood in front of the bombed-out home.

"Oh, my God," she gasped, a hand clasped over her mouth.

Chin led her my way. "Lightower's sister," he said.

She had her hair pulled back tightly, a cashmere sweater over jeans, and a pair of Manolo Blahnik flats I had once mooned over for about ten minutes in the window of Neiman's.

"Please," I said, leading the unsteady woman over to an open black-and-white. "I'm Lieutenant Boxer, Homicide."

"Dianne Aronoff," she muttered vacantly. "I heard it on the news. Mort? Charlotte? The kids . . . Did anyone make it out?"

"We pulled out a boy, about eleven."

"Eric," she said. "He's okay?"

"He's at the Burn Unit at Cal Pacific. I think he's going to be all right."

"Thank God!" she exclaimed. Then she covered her face again. "How can this be happening?"

I knelt down in front of Dianne Aronoff and took her hand. I squeezed it gently. "Ms. Aronoff, I have to ask you some questions. This was no accident. Do you have any idea who could've targeted your brother?"

"No accident," she repeated. "Mortie was saying, 'The media treats me like bin Laden. No one understands. What I do is *supposed* to be about making money.'"

Jacobi switched gears. "Ms. Aronoff, it looks like the explosion originated from the second floor. You have any idea who might've had access to the home?"

"There was a housekeeper," she said, dabbing at her eyes. "Viola."

Jacobi exhaled. "Unfortunately, that's probably the third body we found. Buried under the rubble."

"Oh . . ." Dianne Aronoff choked a sob.

I pressed her hand. "Look, Ms. Aronoff, I

saw the explosion. That bomb was planted from inside. Someone was either let in or had access. I need you to think."

"There was an au pair," she muttered. "I think she sometimes spent the night."

"Lucky for her." Jacobi rolled his eyes. "If she'd been in there with your nephew . . ."

"Not for Eric." Dianne Aronoff shook her head. "For Caitlin."

Jacobi and I looked at each other. "Who?"

"Caitlin, Lieutenant. My niece."

When she saw our blank faces, she froze.

"When you said Eric was the only one brought out, I just assumed . . ."

We continued to stare at each other. No one else had been found in the house.

"Oh, my God, Detectives, she is only six months old."

Chapter 8

This wasn't over.

I ran up to Captain Noroski, the fire chief, who was barking commands to his men searching through the house. "Lightower's sister says there was a six-month-old baby inside."

"No one's inside, Lieutenant. My men are just finishing the upper floor. Unless you wanna go inside and look around again yourself."

Suddenly the layout of the burning building came back to me. I could see it now. Down that same hallway where I'd found the boy. My heart jumped. "Not the upper floors,

Captain, the first." There could've been a nursery down there, too.

Noroski radioed someone still inside the site. He directed him down the front hall.

We stood in front of the smoking house, and a sickening feeling churned in my stomach. The idea of a baby still in there. Someone I could've saved. We waited while Captain Noroski's men picked through the rubble.

Finally, a fireman climbed out from the debris on the ground floor. "Nothing," he called out. "We found the nursery. Crib and a bassinet buried under a lot of rubble. But no baby."

Dianne Aronoff uttered a cry of joy. Her niece wasn't in there. Then a look of panic set in, her face registering a completely new horror. *If Caitlin wasn't there, where was she?*

Chapter 9

Charles Danko stood at the edge of the crowd, watching. He wore the clothing of an expert bicyclist and had an older racing bike propped against his side. If nothing else, the biking helmet and goggles covered his face in case the police were filming the crowd, as they sometimes did.

This couldn't have gone much better, Danko was thinking as he observed the homicide scene. The Lightowers were dead, blown to pieces. He hoped they had suffered greatly as they burned, even the children. This had been a dream of his, or perhaps a nightmare, but now it was reality — and this

particular reality was going to terrify the
good people of San Francisco. This fiery
action had taken nerve on his part, but
finally he'd done something. Look at the firemen, EMS, the local police. They were all
here, in honor of his work, or rather, its humble beginnings.

One of them had caught his eye, a blond
woman, obviously a cop with some clout.
She seemed to have some guts, too. He
watched her and wondered if she would
become his adversary, and would she be
worthy?

He inquired about her from a patrolman at
the barricades. "The woman who went into
the house, that's Inspector Murphy, isn't it? I
think I know her."

The cop didn't even bother to make eye
contact, typical police insolence. "No," he
said, "that's Lieutenant Boxer. She's Homicide. A real bitch on wheels, I hear."

Chapter 10

The cramped third-floor office that housed the Homicide detail was buzzing, unlike any Sunday morning I could remember.

I got a clean bill of health at the hospital, then arrived at the office to find that the whole team had showed up. We had a couple of leads to follow, even before the results of the examination of the blast scene came back. Bombings usually don't involve kidnappings. *Find that baby,* everything told me, *and we'll find whoever did this horrible thing.*

A TV was on. Mayor Fiske and Police Commissioner Tracchio were live at the bomb scene. "This is a horrible, vindictive tragedy," the mayor was saying, having come straight off the first tee at Olympic. "Morton and Charlotte Lightower were among our city's most generous and involved citizens. They were also friends."

"Don't forget contributors," Cappy Thomas, Jacobi's partner, said.

"I want everyone to know that our police department is already vigorously pursuing concrete leads," the mayor continued. "I want to assure the people of this city that this is an isolated event."

"X/L . . ." Warren Jacobi scratched his head. "Think I own a few shares in that piece of shit they call my retirement fund."

"Me too," said Cappy. "Which fund you in?"

"I think it's called Long-Term Growth, but whoever named it sure has a twisted sense of humor. Two years ago I had—"

"If you moguls have a moment," I called. "It's Sunday and the markets are closed. We have three dead, a missing baby, and an entire town house burned to the ground in a possible bombing."

"Definite bombing," Steve Fiori, the department's press liaison, chimed in. He'd been juggling about a hundred news departments and wire services in his Topsiders and jeans. "Chief just got it confirmed from the Bomb Squad. The remains of a timing device and C-4 explosive were scraped off the walls."

The news didn't exactly surprise us. But the realization that a bomb had gone off in our city, that we had murderers out there with C-4, that a six-month-old baby was still missing, sent a numb quiet around the room.

"Shit," Jacobi sighed theatrically, "there goes the afternoon."

Chapter 11

"Lieutenant," someone called from across the room, "Chief Tracchio on the phone."

"Told ya," Cappy said, grinning.

I picked up, waiting to be reamed out for leaving the crime scene early. Tracchio was a glorified bean counter. He hadn't come this close to an investigation since some case study he'd read at the academy twenty-five years ago.

"Lindsay, it's Cindy." I'd been expecting to hear the Chief; her voice surprised me. "Don't get cranky. It was the only way I could get through."

"Not exactly a good time," I said. "I thought

you were that asshole Tracchio, about to nail me to the wall."

"Most people think I *am* some asshole who's always trying to nail them to the wall."

"This one signs my checks," I said, taking a semirelaxed breath for the first time all day.

Cindy Thomas was part of my inner circle, along with Claire and Jill. She also happened to work for the *Chronicle* and was one of the top crime reporters in the city.

"Jesus, Linds, I just heard. I'm in an all-day yoga clinic. In the middle of a 'downward dog' when my phone rings. What, I sneak out for a couple of hours and you decide now's the time to be a hero? You all right?"

"Other than my lungs feeling like they've been lit with lighter fluid . . . No, I'm okay," I said. "There's not much I can tell you on this now."

"I'm not calling about the crime scene, Lindsay. I was calling about *you*."

"I'm okay," I said again. I didn't know if I was telling the truth. I noticed that my hands were still trembling. And my mouth tasted the bitter smoke of the blast.

"You want me to meet you?"

"You wouldn't get within two blocks. Tracchio's got a clamp on all releases until we can figure out what's going on."

"Is that a challenge?" Cindy snickered.

That made me laugh. When I first met her, Cindy had sneaked her way into a Grand Hyatt penthouse suite, the most guarded murder scene in memory. Her whole career sprang from that scoop.

"No, it's not a challenge, Cindy. But I'm okay. I swear."

"Okay, so if all this tender concern is being wasted, what *about* the crime scene? We are talking a crime scene, aren't we, Lindsay?"

"If you mean, did the backyard grill flare up at nine on a Sunday morning? Yeah, I guess you could quote me on that. I thought you were out of touch on this, Cindy." It always amazed me how quickly she got herself up to speed.

"I'm on it now," she said. "And while I'm at it, word is that you saved a kid today. You should go home. You've done enough for one day."

"Can't. We got a few leads. Wish I could talk about them, but I can't."

"I heard there was a baby stolen out of the house. Some sort of twisted kidnapping?"

"If it is," I said with a shrug, "they have a new way of handling the potential ransom payers."

Cappy Thomas stuck his head in. "Lieutenant, M.E. wants to see you. In the morgue. Now."

Chapter 12

Leave it to Claire, San Francisco's chief medical officer, my best friend of a dozen years, to say the one thing in the midst of this madness that would make me cry. "Charlotte Lightower was pregnant."

Claire was looking drawn and helpless in her orange surgical scrubs. "Two months. Poor woman probably didn't even know herself."

I don't know why I found that so sad, but I did. Maybe it made the Lightowers seem like more of a family to me, humanized them.

"I was hoping to catch up with you sometime today." Claire gave me a halfhearted smile. "Just didn't envision it like this."

"Yeah." I smiled and wiped a tear from the corner of my eye.

"I heard what you did," Claire said. She came over and gave me a hug. "That took a lot of guts, honey. Also, you are a dumb bunny, do you know that?"

"There was a moment when I wasn't sure I was going to make it out, Claire. There was all this smoke. It was everywhere. In my eyes, my lungs. I couldn't see for shit. I just took hold of that little boy and prayed."

"You saw the light. It led you out?" Claire smiled.

"No. Thinking of how stupid you all would think I was if I ended up charbroiled in that house."

"Woulda put a bit of a damper on our margarita nights," she said, nodding.

"Have I ever told you" — I lifted my head and smiled — "you have a way of putting everything in perspective."

The Lightowers' remains were side by side on two gurneys. Even at Christmas the morgue is a lonely place, but on that Sunday afternoon, with the techs gone home, graphic autopsy photos and medical alerts pinned to the antiseptic walls, and a grisly smell in the air, it was as grim as I could remember.

I moved over to the bodies.

"So, you called me down here," I said. "What did you want me to see?"

"I called you down here," she said, "'cause it occurred to me that you needed a good hug."

"I did," I said, "but a killer medical revelation wouldn't hurt."

Claire moved over to a table and started to take off her surgical gloves. "Killer medical revelation?" She rolled her eyes. "What could I possibly have for you, Lindsay. These three people, they were blown up."

Chapter 13

An hour later Tracchio and I held a tense, very emotional news briefing on the steps of the Hall. Cindy was there, along with about half the city's news force.

Back in the office, Jacobi had run the name on the photo, August Spies, through the CCI database and the FBI. It came back zilch. No match on any name or group. Cappy was digging up whatever he could on the missing au pair. We had a description from Lightower's sister, but no idea how to find her. She didn't even know the girl's last name.

I took a thick Bell Western Yellow Pages

off a shelf and tossed it with a loud *thump* on Cappy's desk. "Here, start with N, for nannies."

It was almost six o'clock on Sunday. We had a team down at X/L's offices, but the best we could get was a corporate public relations flack who said we could meet with them tomorrow at 8 A.M. Sundays were shit crime-solving days.

Jacobi and Cappy knocked on my door. "Why don't you go on home?" Cappy said. "We'll handle it from here."

"I was just gonna buzz Charlie Clapper." His CSU team was still picking through the scene.

"I mean it, Lindsay. We got you covered. You look like shit, anyway," Jacobi said.

Suddenly I realized just how exhausted I was. It had been nine hours since the town house had blown. I was still in a sweatshirt and running gear. The grime of the blast was all over me.

"Hey, LT." Cappy turned back. "Just one more thing. How did it go last night with Franklin Fratelli? Your big date?"

They were standing there, chewing on their grin like two oversize teenagers. "It didn't," I said. "Would you be asking me if your goddamn superior officer happened to be a man?"

"Damn right, I'd be askin'," Cappy said. "And might I add, for my goddamn superior officer"—the big detective threw his bald head back—"you're looking mighty fine here in those tights. That Fratelli brother, he must be quite a fool."

"Noted." I smiled. It had taken me a long time to feel in charge of these guys. Both of them had double my time on the force. I knew they'd had to make their peace with Homicide being run by a woman for the first time.

"Something you want to add to that, Warren?" I asked.

"Nope." He rocked on his heels. "Only, we doin' suits and ties tomorrow, or can I wear my tennis shorts and Nikes?"

I brushed past him, shaking my head. Then I heard my name one more time. "Lieutenant?"

I turned, piqued. "Warren?"

"You did good today." He nodded. "The ones who matter know."

Chapter 14

It was only a ten-minute drive out to Potrero, where I live in a two-bedroom walk-up. As I went through my door, Martha wagged up to me. One of the patrolmen at the scene had taken her home for me.

The message light was flashing. Jill's voice: "Lindsay, I tried to call you at the office. I just heard. . . ." Fratelli: "Listen, Lindsay, if you're free today . . ." I deleted it without even hearing what he had to say for himself.

I went into the bedroom and peeled off my tights and sweats. I didn't want to talk to anyone tonight. I flicked on a CD. The Reverend

Al Green. I stepped into the shower and took a swig of a beer I'd brought with me. I leaned back under the warming spray, the grit and soot and smell of ash chipping off my body, swirling at my feet. Something made me feel like crying.

I felt so alone.

I could've died today.

I wished I had someone's arms to slide into.

Claire had Edmund to soothe her on a night like tonight, after she pieced three charred bodies together. Jill had Steve, whatever . . . Even Martha had someone — me!

I felt my thoughts drift to Chris for the first time in a while. It would be nice if he were here tonight. It had been eighteen months since he died. I was ready to put it behind me, to open myself to someone, if someone happened to be on the scene. No drumroll. No "Ladies and gentlemen, the envelope, please. . . ." Just this little voice in my heart, my voice, telling me it was time.

Then I drifted back to the scene at the Marina. I saw myself on the street, holding Martha. The beautiful, calm morning; the stucco town house. The redheaded kid spinning his Razor. The flash of orange light.

Over and over I ran the reel, and it kept ending at the same point.

There's something you're not seeing. Something I had edited out.

The woman turning the corner just before the flash. I had seen only a glimpse of her back. Blond, ponytail. Something in her arms. But that wasn't what was bothering me.

It was that she never came back.

I hadn't thought about it until now. After the blast . . . The kid with the Razor was there. Lots of others. But the blond woman wasn't among them. No one interviewed her. She never came back . . . Why?

Because the son of a bitch was running away.

That moment flashed over and over in my mind. Something in her arms. She was running away.

It was the au pair.

And the bundle in her arms?

That was the Lightowers' baby!

Chapter 15

Her hair fell in thick, blond clumps onto the bathroom floor. She took the scissors and cut again. Everything had to start over now. Wendy was gone forever. A new face began to emerge in the mirror. She said good-bye to the au pair she had been for the past five months.

Cut away the past. Wendy was a name for Peter Pan, not the real world.

The baby was screaming in the bedroom. "Hush, Caitlin. Please, honey."

She had to figure it out—what to do with her. All she knew was that she couldn't let the baby die. She had listened to the news reports all afternoon. The whole world was looking for her. They were calling her a cold-blooded killer. A monster. But she couldn't be such a monster, could she? Not if she had saved the baby.

"You don't think I'm such a monster, do you, Caitlin?" she called to the bawling child.

Michelle lowered her head into the sink and dumped a bottle of L'Oréal Red Sunset dye all over her, massaging it into her cropped hair.

Wendy, the au pair, disappeared.

Any moment now, Malcolm would come by. They had agreed not to meet until they were sure she hadn't been followed. But she needed him. Now that she'd proved what she was made of.

She heard the sound of the front door being rattled. Michelle's heart jumped.

What if she'd been careless? What if someone had seen her coming back with the kid? What if they were kicking the door down now!

Then Malcolm stepped into the room. "You were expecting cops, weren't you? I *told* you they're stupid!" he said. Michelle ran over to him and jumped into his arms.

"Oh, Mal, we did it. We did it." She kissed

his face about a hundred times. "I did the right thing, didn't I?" Michelle asked. "I mean, the TV is saying that whoever did this was a monster."

"I told you, you have to be strong, Michelle." Mal stroked her hair. "The TV, they're bought and paid for, just like the rest. But look at you. . . . You look so different."

Suddenly, there was a cry from the bedroom. Mal took a gun from his belt. "What the fuck was that?"

She was behind him as he ran into the bedroom. He stared, horrified, at Caitlin.

"Mal, we can keep her, just for a little while. I'll care for her. She's done nothing wrong."

"You dumb twit," he said, pushing her onto the bed. "Every cop in the city will be looking for this kid."

She felt herself wheezing now. The way she always did when Mal's voice got hard. She fumbled around her purse for her inhaler. It was always there. She never went anywhere without it. She'd had it just last night. *Where the hell was it now?*

"I cared for her, Malcolm," Michelle said again. "I thought you'd understand. . . ."

Malcolm pushed her face in front of the

child. "Yeah, well understand *this*. . . . That kid is gone, *tomorrow*. You make it stop crying. Stick your tits in its mouth, put a fucking pillow over its head. In the morning, the baby's gone."

Chapter 16

Charles Danko didn't believe in taking unnecessary chances; he also resolutely believed that all soldiers were expendable, even himself. He had always preached the gospel: *there's always another soldier.*

So he made the call from a pay phone in the Mission District. If the call was interrupted, if the call was discovered, well, so be it.

The phone rang several times before someone picked up at the apartment. He recognized the voice of Michelle, the wonderfully coldhearted au pair. What a performance she'd put on.

"I'm proud of you, Michelle. Please don't say anything. Just put Malcolm on. You are a hero, though."

Michelle put the phone down, and Danko had to choke back a laugh at how they obeyed his orders.

It was priceless and it said so much about the human condition. Hell, it might even explain Hitler at Munich. These were very smart people, most of them with graduate degrees, but they rarely questioned anything he told them.

"Yeah. It's me."

He heard Malcolm's cheerless voice. This boy was brilliant, but he was truly a killer, probably a psychopath; he even scared Danko sometimes.

"Listen to me. I don't want to stay on too long. I just wanted to give you an update — everything is working beautifully. It couldn't be better."

Danko paused for a couple of seconds. "Do it again," he finally said.

Chapter 17

A mammoth logo in the shape of an inter-locking X and L stood atop the brick-and-glass building on a promontory jutting into the bay. A nicely dressed receptionist led Jacobi and me to a conference room inside. On the paneled walls, articles and magazine covers featuring Morton Lightower's glowing face ran the length of the room. One *Forbes* cover asked, CAN ANYONE IN SILICON VALLEY STOP THIS MAN?

"Just what does this company do?" I asked Jacobi.

"High-speed switches or something. They move data over the Internet. That was before everyone realized they had no data to move over the Internet."

The door to the conference room opened and two men stepped in. One had salt-and-pepper hair and a ruddy complexion, a well-cut suit. Lawyer. The other, heavy and balding, with an open plaid shirt. Tech.

"Chuck Zinn," the suit introduced himself, offering a card to Jacobi. "I'm X/L's CLO. You're Lieutenant Boxer?"

"*I'm* Lieutenant Boxer." I stared at the card and sniffed. "What's a CLO?"

"Chief legal officer." He bowed apologetically. "This is Gerry Cates, who helped found the company with Mort.

"Needless to say, we're horrified around here." The two men took seats, as we did, around the conference table. "Most of us have known Mort since the beginning. Gerry went to Berkeley with him. I want to start by promising the full cooperation of the company."

"Are there any leads?" Cates inquired. "We've heard Caitlin is missing."

"We're doing everything we can to follow up on the baby. We were told the family had an au pair—who's missing. Any help you could give in finding her?"

"Maybe Helene could help you out. Mort's secretary." Cates looked at the lawyer.

"I think that's doable." Zinn scratched a note.

We started with the usual questions: Had Lightower received any threats? Were they aware of anyone who'd want to do him harm?

"No." Gerry Cates shook his head and glanced at the lawyer. "Of course, Mort's financial affairs were paraded all over the media," he continued. "People are always popping off at shareholder meetings. Financial watchdogs. Hell, you want to redo your kitchen, they're crying you're bleeding the company."

Jacobi sniffed. "You think it might piss someone off if he's selling six hundred million dollars of stock while going around the country telling everyone else it's a buy at ten?"

"We can't control our share price, Inspector," Cates replied, clearly upset by the question.

A tense silence settled over the room.

"You'll provide us a list of all your clients," I said.

"Doable." The lawyer jotted down a note again.

"And we'll need access to his private computers, e-mail, and correspondence." I lobbed a grenade at the CLO.

The lawyer's pen never touched the page. "Those files are private, Lieutenant. I think I'd better check our legal footing before I can agree to that."

"I thought you were the legal footing," Jacobi said with a grin.

"Your boss has been murdered, Mr. Zinn. I'm afraid they're our matters now. There was a note at the bomb scene," I said. I pushed across a copy of the photo. "It referred to Morton Lightower as an 'enemy of the people.' There's a name at the bottom, August Spies. Mean anything to either of you?"

Zinn blinked. Cates took a deep breath, his eyes suddenly blank.

"I don't need to remind you that this is a murder investigation," I said. "If anyone's holding something back, now would be the time . . ."

"No one's holding anything back," Gerry Cates said stiffly.

"You probably want to talk to Helene now." The CLO straightened his pad, as if the meeting was over.

"What I *want* is Lightower's office sealed,

now. And I want access to all correspondence. Computer files as well. And e-mail."

"I'm not sure that's doable, Lieutenant." Chuck Zinn arched back in his chair.

"Let me tell you what's doable, Mr. Zinn." I fastened on his phony, compliant grin. "What's doable is that we're back here in two hours with a subpoena, and anything deleted from those files in the past twenty-four hours goes under the heading of impeding a murder investigation. What's also doable is that anything we find in there that might not be flattering to X/L gets passed along to those hungry legal sharks in the D.A.'s office. Any of that sound *doable,* Mr. Zinn?"

Gerry Cates leaned toward his lawyer. "Chuck, maybe we could work something out."

"Of course we can work something out." Zinn nodded. "But I'm afraid that's all we have time for today. And you must be busy as well. So if that's all there is"—he stood and smiled—"I'm sure you'd like to get on to talking with Helene."

Chapter 18

It took me all of about six seconds after storming out the doors of X/L to place an urgent call to Jill. I took her through the frustrating meeting I'd just come out of.

"You're looking for a subpoena," Jill cut me off, "to get into Lightower's files?"

"Duh, Jill, and fast, before they send in the Arthur Andersen boys to do a little office tidying."

"Any evidence there's anything in Lightower's computer to back that up?"

"Call me suspicious, Jill, but when a guy I'm interviewing starts to twist around like a cod on a fishing line, those little police antennae behind my ears always go *twang*."

"How do they go, Lindsay?" Jill chuckled back.

"Twang," I said, more firmly. "C'mon, Jill, I'm not screwing around."

"Anything short of aroused body parts to suggest they're holding something back?"

The blood began to roil in my chest. "You're not gonna do this for me, are you?"

"I *can't* do this for you, Lindsay. And if I did, whatever you found wouldn't make it through arraignment. Look, I could try to cut a deal with them."

"Jill. I've got a multiple-murder investigation."

"Then if I were you, I'd try to apply some nonlegal pressure."

"You want to spell that out for me?"

Jill snorted. "Last I checked, you still had a few friends in the news media. . . ."

"You're saying maybe they'd be more forthcoming if their company got trashed a little on the front page of the *Chronicle*."

"Duh, Linds . . ." I heard Jill giggle.

All of a sudden a beep sounded on my cell phone.

Cappy Thomas at the office. "Lieutenant, I need you back at home base, posthaste. We got a line on the au pair."

Chapter 19

Two women were sitting in Interrogation Room 1 when I got back. They owned a small placement service for nannies and au pairs, Cappy informed me. "A Nanny Is Love!"

"We called in when we heard about what happened," Linda Cliborne, in a pink cashmere sweater, explained to me. "We placed Wendy Raymore in that job."

"She seemed perfect for it," her partner, Judith Hertan, jumped in. Judith took out a yellow file and pushed it across the table. Inside was a filled-out A Nanny Is Love! application form, a couple of letters of recommendation, a Cal-Berkeley student ID with a photo on it.

"The Lightowers adored her," Linda said.

I stared at the small laminated photo of Wendy Raymore's face. She was blond with high cheekbones, a wide, blossoming smile. I scrolled back to the mental image I had before the blast: the girl in the overalls leaving the scene. This could be her.

"We carefully screen all of our girls. Wendy seemed like a gem. She was cheerful and attractive, a totally likable kid."

"And the Lightowers said their little baby had taken to her like honey," her partner added. "We always check."

"These recommendations . . . you checked them, too?"

Judith Hertan hesitated. "We may not have followed up on all of them. I did check with the school, made sure she was in good standing. We had her college ID, of course."

I fixed on the address: 17 Pelican Drive. Across the bay in Berkeley.

"I think she said she lived off-campus," Linda Cliborne said. "We mailed her confirmation to a post office box."

I took Cappy and Jacobi outside the room. "I'll alert the Berkeley PD. And Tracchio."

"How do you want to handle it?" Cappy looked at me. What he meant was, *What kind of force should we use to pick her up?*

I stared at the photo.

"Use everything," I said.

Chapter 20

Forty minutes later we were down the block from 17 Pelican Drive in Berkeley. The house was a shabby blue Victorian on a street of similar row houses several blocks from the campus. Two patrol cars had the street blocked off. A SWAT van pulled up alongside. I didn't know what to expect, but I wasn't taking any chances.

We all donned protective vests under our police jackets. It was 11:45. The Berkeley PD had the house under surveillance. They said no one had left, but a black girl carrying a Cal-Berkeley bag had gone in thirty minutes before.

"Let's go find a missing baby," I said to the guys.

Jacobi, Cappy, and I crept behind a line of parked cars close to the front of the house. No sign of activity inside. We knew the place could be booby-trapped.

Two inspectors sidled up to the front porch. A SWAT team guy waited with a ram in case we needed to break in. The scene was eerily quiet.

I gave the nod. *Let's go in.*

"Open up! San Francisco Police!" Cappy rapped heavily on the door.

My eyes were peeled to the side windows for any sign of activity. They had already used a bomb. I was sure there'd be no hesitation to opening up with guns. But there was nothing.

Suddenly, I heard footsteps approaching from inside, the sound of a lock being turned. As the door swung open, we trained our guns on whoever was behind it.

The black girl in a Cal-Berkeley sweatshirt, whom the Berkeley cops had seen going in. One look at the SWAT team and she let out a startled scream.

"Wendy Raymore?" Cappy barked, yanking her out of the doorway.

The shocked girl could barely speak. Cappy threw her into the arms of a waiting SWAT team member. Trembling, she pointed to a staircase. "I think she's up there."

The three of us pushed our way inside. Two upstairs bedrooms were open and empty. No one inside. Down the hall, another door was closed.

Cappy rapped at the door. "Wendy Raymore? San Francisco Police!"

There was no answer.

The adrenaline was burning in my veins. Cappy looked at me and checked his gun. Jacobi readied himself. I nodded.

Cappy kicked open the door. We moved in, leveling guns around the room.

A girl in a T-shirt shot up in bed. She looked stunned, blinking sleep from her eyes. She started to shriek: "Oh, my God, what's going on?"

"Wendy Raymore?" Cappy kept his gun on her.

The girl's face was white with terror, eyes going back and forth.

"Where's the baby?" Cappy shouted.

This is all wrong! Fucking all wrong, I was thinking.

The girl had long dark hair and a swarthy

complexion. She looked nothing like the description Dianne Aronoff had given us. Or the picture on Wendy Raymore's student ID. Or the girl I saw hurrying away from the bombing. I thought I knew what had happened. This girl had probably lost her ID, or it had been stolen. But who had it now?

I put down my gun. We were staring at a different girl.

"This isn't the au pair," I said.

Chapter 21

Lucille Cleamons had exactly seventeen minutes left on her lunch hour to wipe the ketchup stain off Marcus's face, get the twins to the day care clinic, and catch the 27 bus back to work before Mr. Darmon would start docking her $7.85 per hour (or 13 cents a minute).

"*C'mon,* Marcus," she sighed to her five-year-old, who was sprouting a face full of ketchup. "I don't have time for this today." She dabbed at his white, collared dress shirt, which had taken on the look of one of his messier finger paintings, and—damn—none of the stain was coming off.

Cherisse pointed from her chair. "Can I have an ice cream, Momma?"

"No, child, you can't. Momma's got no time." She looked at her watch and felt her heart stab. *Oh God . . .*

"C'mon, child." Lucille crammed their Happy Meal boxes onto the tray. "I got to get you cleaned up fast."

"Please, Momma, it's a McSundae," Cherisse cried.

"You can buy your own McSundae or whatever you like when it's your dollar sixty-five going across the table. Now both you come get yourselves cleaned up. Momma's got to go."

"But I am clean," Cherisse protested.

She dragged them out of the booth and hurried toward the bathroom. "Yes, but your brother looks like he's been in a war."

Lucille pulled her kids along the back corridor leading to the bathrooms. She opened the door to the ladies' room. It was McDonald's. No one would mind. She raised Marcus on the counter and wet a paper towel and started to rub at the mess on his collar.

The boy squirmed.

"Damn, child, you want to make the mess,

you got to own up to the cleaning. Cherisse, you got to pee?"

"Yes, Momma," the girl replied.

She was the cleaner of the two. They were both five, but Marcus barely knew how to pull down his own zipper. Some of the ketchup was starting to come off.

"Cherisse," Lucille barked, "you going to get on that toilet seat, or what?"

"Can't, Momma," the child replied.

"*Can't?* Who's got time for this, young lady? Just drop your stockings and pee."

"I can't, Momma. You gotta come see."

Lucille sighed. Whoever said time is on your side sure never had twins. She took a quick glance in the mirror, sighing again, not ever a single second for herself. She helped Marcus to the floor, then went to open Cherisse's stall.

She said impatiently, "So what you crying about, child?"

The little girl was staring at the toilet.

"My God." Lucille took a breath.

On the toilet seat, wrapped in a blanket in a bassinet, was an infant.

Chapter 22

Once in a while there are moments in this job when everything works out for you. Finding the Lightower baby at McDonald's was one of those times. The entire Hall seemed to breathe a deep, grateful sigh of relief.

I got Cindy on the line and asked a favor. She said she'd be delighted to put a little pressure on X/L.

I hung up with Cindy, and Charlie Clapper was knocking on my door. "Nice bust, Boxer."

"That's a little sexist, even from you," I said with a smile.

Clapper laughed. His Crime Scene team had spent the better part of the past day and a half picking through the bomb site. Charlie looked exhausted.

"FYEF, darlin'," he said, motioning with his head for me to follow. "For your eyes first. They're a whole lot cuter than Tracchio's."

"Knew I earned this gold shield for something."

Charlie took me to his office down the hall. Niko was in there, from the Bomb Squad, leaning back in Charlie's old hardwood recliner and picking something out of a Chinese food container.

"Okay, we've pieced together an idea of the explosive device." Charlie threw out a chair for me. On a poster board, someone had drawn a floor plan of the Lightowers' town house. "Traces of C-4 were all over the place. Half a pound's enough to blow a jet from the sky, so from the size of the blast, I figure this was about five times that. Whoever did it put it inside something like this" —he took out a black Nike sport bag—"and placed it in one of the rooms."

"How do we know that?" I asked.

"Easy." Clapper grinned. He pulled out a fragment of black nylon with a Nike swoosh on it. "We found this plastered against the wall."

"Any luck you could scrape a few prints off the bag?" I asked hopefully.

"Sorry, honey," Clapper snickered, "this *is* the bag."

"It was triggered by a fairly sophisticated device," Niko explained. "Remote detonation. Blasting cap was hooked up to a cell phone."

"There's a market for C-4, Lindsay. We could look into any construction-site thefts, missing military inventory," said Charlie Clapper.

"How are you with babies, Charlie?"

"If they're eighteen or over," the CSU man said, grinning. "Why? You finally getting the itch?"

If Clapper were a foot taller, fifty pounds lighter, and hadn't been married for thirty years, I just might take him up on his little flirtations one day. "Sorry, this one's a little younger."

"You mean the Lightower baby?" Charlie scrunched his face.

I nodded. "I want her dusted, Charlie. The kid, blanket, bassinet, anything you can find."

"Been thirty years since I changed a diaper." Clapper let out a breath, looking a little squeamish. "Hey, I almost forgot. . . ." He pulled out a coded evidence bag from underneath a pile of papers on the desk. "There was a room down the hall from the nursery. Someone spent the night there. Someone who isn't accounted for now."

The au pair, I was thinking.

"Don't get excited," Charlie said, shrugging. "Everything was cinders. But we picked up this by the bed."

He tossed me the plastic bag. Inside was a small, twisted canister about three inches long.

I held it up. Didn't have the slightest idea what it was.

"Everything must've melted." Clapper shrugged. He fumbled behind him through his jacket draped over the chair. He came out with something that looked similar.

"Proventil, Lindsay." He took the cap off his own device and fit it neatly onto the one from the evidence bag. He pressed the mouthpiece twice. Two puffs shot out into the air.

"Whoever slept in that bed had asthma."

Chapter 23

Jill Bernhardt sat in her darkened office long after everyone else had left.

A law brief was open in front of her, and she suddenly realized she'd been staring at the same page for ten minutes now. On nights when Steve wasn't traveling or working late, she had taken to staying at the office. Doing anything she could to avoid him. Even when she wasn't preparing for trial.

Jill Meyer Bernhardt. Superlawyer. Everybody's alpha dog.

She was afraid to go home.

Slowly, she massaged the bruise on her backbone. The newest bruise. How could

this be happening? She was used to repre-
senting women who felt like this, not hiding a
secret in the dark herself.

A tear wound its way down her cheek. *It
was when I lost the baby,* she thought. That's
when it all started.

But, no, the trouble with Steve had started
long before that, she knew. When she was
just out of law school and he was finishing up
his MBA. It started with what she would wear.
Outfits that weren't his taste or showed her
scars. Dinner parties where his opinion—
politics, her job, anything—seemed so much
stronger, more important than hers. Pretending it was his earnings that had paid for the
down payment on the town house, the
Beemer.

You can't do it, Jill. She had heard that
since she met him. Jesus Christ, she
dabbed her eyes with the heel of her hands.
She was the top assistant D.A. in the city.
What else did she have to prove?

The phone rang. The sudden ring made
her jump. Was it Steve? Just the sound of
his voice made her sick. That creepy, oh-
so-concerned, oh-so-solicitous tone: "Hey,
honey, watchya doin'? Come on home. Let's
take a run."

To her relief, the caller ID said it was an assistant D.A. from Sacramento. He was calling back on getting a witness cleared out of a state pen. She let it go to her voice mail.

She closed the heavy brief. This was the last time, she vowed. She would start by telling Lindsay. It hurt her not to be honest with her. Lindsay thought Steve was a prick anyway. She was no fool.

As she was stuffing her briefcase, the phone rang again. This time it had that special ring, cutting right through her.

Don't answer, Jill. She was already halfway out the door. But something made her look at the digital screen. The familiar number lit up. Jill felt her mouth go dry. Slowly, she picked up the receiver. "Bernhardt," she whispered, closing her eyes.

"Working late again, hon?" Steve's voice cut through her. "If I didn't know better," he said, sounding almost hurt, "I'd think you were afraid to come home."

Chapter 24

That night, George Bengosian got lucky.

Short and balding, with a large flattened nose, Bengosian had realized early in his residency that he had no flair for urology and found his true calling stringing together failing regional insurers into giant HMOs. He also realized he wasn't the type who could charm a beautiful woman with his profit projections and silly industry jokes—certainly not this sexy analyst at the Bank of America Health Care Conference.

It was as if he were living someone else's dream. Mimi was mesmerized by him, and now they were on the way to his suite. "The penthouse, wait until you see the view," he teased.

George giddily traced the outline of her bra as he opened the door to his suite at the Clift; he was imagining her perky tits jiggling in front of him, and those mooning eyes staring into his. This was what having your picture in the annual report was all about.

"Give me just a second," Mimi said, pinching his arm and heading into the powder room.

"Not too long," George said with a pout.

In clumsy haste, he ripped the wrapping off a bottle of Roederer that had come complimentary with the suite and poured out two glasses. His fifty-four-year-old cock flopped around in his pants like a cod in a catch basket. In the morning he had to be back in the jet, off to a meeting of the Illinois Senate Health Care Committee, which he already knew had been swayed into looking the other way while he dropped the poorest individual accounts and highest risks from his enrollment. One hundred forty thousand families out of the plan, and all of it accretive to the bottom line!

Mimi came back from the powder room,

and she looked better than ever. George handed her a glass.

"To you," he said. "Well, to both of us. To tonight."

"To Hopewell." Mimi flashed a smile and clinked glasses.

"Hey, want to try something?" She put her hand on his wrist. "This is guaranteed to make your projections *rock-solid firm.*" She produced a vial from her purse. "Just stick out your tongue."

George did as he was told, and she dribbled out two drops.

Bitter. The taste was so sharp, it almost made him jump. "Can't they make these things in cherry flavor?"

"One more." Her smile was dazzling. "Just to make sure you're ready for me. For *us.*"

George stuck out his tongue again. His heart was beating out of control.

Mimi dribbled out another drop. Then her smile changed. Colder. She squeezed him by the cheeks, turned the entire vial upside down.

George's mouth filled with the liquid. He tried to spit it out, but she threw his head back and he swallowed. His eyes popped. "What the hell?"

"It's toxic," Mimi said, tossing the empty vial back into her purse. "Very special poison for a very special guy. The first drop would be enough to kill you in a few hours. You just swallowed enough to waste San Francisco."

George's champagne glass dropped and shattered on the floor. He tried to spit the ingested liquid back out. This bitch must be insane. She must be screwing with him. But then a violent pain shook his abdomen.

"This is from all those people you've spent your life fucking, Mr. Bengosian. No one you've ever met, just families who had no choice in life but to count on you. On Hopewell. Felicia Brown? She died of treatable melanoma. Thomas Ortiz? Name ring a bell? It would to your risk-management team. He shot himself trying to pay off his son's brain tumor. We call it 'cleaning the coffers.' Isn't that what you say, Mr. B?"

Suddenly his stomach began to wrench. A viscous froth built up in his mouth. He spit it out, all over his shirt, but it was as if sharp, clawing fingers were tearing at the lining of his gut. He knew what was taking place. Pulmonary edema. Instant organ failure. *Yell for help,* he told himself. *Get to the door.* But his legs gave out, crumbling beneath him.

Mimi was standing there, watching him with a mocking grin. He reached out in her direction. He wanted to hit her, squeeze her throat, crush the life out of her. But he couldn't move.

"Please . . ." This was no joke.

She knelt over him. "How does it feel to have your coffers cleaned, Mr. Bengosian? Now be a dear and open your mouth one more time. Open wide!"

With all his might George tried to suck air into his lungs, but there was nothing. His jaw fell open. His tongue had swelled to a monstrous size. Mimi held a blue piece of paper in front of his face. At least he thought it was blue—but his eyes were refractive and glassy and weren't registering colors very well. In the blurry outline he saw Hopewell's logo.

She crumpled the paper into a ball and shoved it in his mouth. "Thanks for thinking of Hopewell, but as the form says, coverage is denied!"

Chapter 25

My cell phone was beeping.

It was the middle of the night. I shot up and blinked at the clock. *Shit, 4 A.M.*

Groggily, I fumbled for the phone, trying to read the number on the screen. It was Paul Chin's. "Hey, Paul, what's going on?" I mumbled.

"Sorry, LT, I'm at the Clift Hotel. I'm thinking you better come on down."

"You find something?" A four-in-the-morning question? Four-in-the-morning calls meant only one thing.

"Yeah. I think the Lightower bombing just got a bit more complicated."

Eight minutes later—jeans and a tank thrown on, and a few purposeful brushes through my hair—I was in the Explorer, bounding down Vermont on the way to Seventh, top hat flashing through the quiet night.

Three black-and-whites along with a morgue van were crowded around the hotel's bright new entrance. The Clift was one of the city's great old hotels and had just undergone a fancy renovation. I badged my way past the cops at the front, gawking at the lavish ostrich-hide couch and bulls' horns on the wall, a few stunned hotel employees standing around, wondering what to do. I took the elevator up to the top floor, where Chin was waiting.

"The vic's name is George Bengosian. Health-care bigwig," Paul Chin explained as he led me into the penthouse suite. "Prepare yourself. I'm not kidding."

I looked at the body, propped upright against the leg of a conference table in the lavishly appointed room.

The color of Bengosian's skin had turned a hypoxic green-yellow, the consistency of jelly. His eyes were wrenched open like mangled gear sockets. Mucus, or some sort of viscous orange fluid, ran out of his nose and had caked grotesquely on his chin.

"What the hell did he do," I muttered to the med tech leaning over him, "get into a life-sucking contest with an alien?"

The tech looked totally mystified. "I don't have the slightest idea."

"You're sure this is a *homicide?*" I turned to Chin.

"Front desk got a call, two forty-five A.M.," he said with a shrug, "from outside the hotel. Said there was some garbage that needed to be picked up in the penthouse."

"Works for me." I sniffled.

"That, and *this,*" Chin said, producing a balled-up piece of paper that he picked up with latex gloves. "Found it in his mouth."

It looked like some kind of crumpled business form.

A white embossed logo: Hopewell Health Care.

It was a statement of benefits. Some text filled in. As I started to read, my blood ran cold.

We have declared war on the agents of greed and corruption in our society. No longer can we sit back and tolerate the powered class, whose only birthright is arrogance, as they enrich them-selves on the oppressed, the weak, and the poor. The era of economic apartheid is over. We will find you, no matter how large your house or powerful your lawyers. We are inside your homes, your workplaces. We announce to you, your war is not beyond, but here. It is with us.

Oh fuck. I looked at Chin. This wasn't a homicide. It was an execution. A declaration of war. And he was right, the Lightower bombing did just get a lot more complicated.

The note was signed, August Spies.

Part Two

Chapter 26

My first call was to Claire.

We had about an hour. That was all we had before this grotesque, seemingly random murder became headlines around the world as the second killing in a vicious terror spree. I needed to know how Bengosian had died, and fast.

The second call was to Tracchio. It was still before five A.M. The night duty officer patched me through.

"It's Lindsay Boxer," I said. "You said to make sure you knew the minute something went on."

"Yeah," I heard him grunt, fumbling around with the phone.

"I'm at the Clift Hotel. I think we just found the motive for the Lightower bombing."

I could visualize him bolting upright in his pajamas, knocking his glasses onto the floor. "One of those X/L partners finally come clean? It was money, wasn't it?"

"No," I said, shaking my head, *"war."*

After I hung up with the Chief, I looked around Bengosian's hotel room. No blood, no sign of a struggle. A half-filled champagne glass rested on the conference table. Another shattered, at Bengosian's feet. His suit jacket was thrown onto the couch. An open bottle of Roederer.

"Get a description of who he came up with," I told Lorraine Stafford, one of my Homicide inspectors. "They might have security cameras in the lobby if we're lucky. And let's try and track down how Bengosian spent the early part of his night."

We have declared war, the note read, *on the agents of greed and corruption. . . .*

A chill went right through me. *It was going to happen again.*

I knew that in the next few hours I had to find out everything I could about Bengosian and Hopewell Health Care. I had no idea what he had done to be murdered like this.

I picked up the crumpled note.

We will find you, no matter how large your house or powerful your lawyers. We are inside your homes, your workplaces. . . . Your war is not beyond, but here. It is with us.

Who the hell are you, August Spies?

Chapter 27

By the time most people were turning on the morning news, we had descriptions of a "cute brunette in a suit" (the night doorman) who "looked like she was totally into him" (their waiter at Masa's) and had accompanied Bengosian back to his room last night.

She was either the killer or an accomplice who had let the killer in. A different girl from the one we were seeking as the au pair.

I looked up from the papers on my desk and saw Claire. "Got a second, Lindsay?"

Claire always maintained an upbeat side, even in the grimmest of cases, but it was clear from her expression that she didn't like what she had found. "I owe you a couple of hours sleep," I said.

Her worried eyes said, *No, you don't.*

"I've been doing this work ten years." Claire sank into the chair across my desk and shook her head. "I've never seen the inside of a body that looked like that."

"I'm listening," I said, leaning forward.

"I don't even know what to call it," she said. "It was like jelly in there. Total vascular and pulmonary collapse. Hemorrhaging all through the gastrointestinal tract. Massive splenetic and renal necrosis . . . *Degradation,* Lindsay," she said, seeing my eyes glaze.

I shrugged. "We talking some kind of poison, Claire?"

"Yeah, but with a toxicity that's way beyond anything I've seen before. I skimmed through a few journals. I once worked on this child who had a similar vascular collapse and edema; we tied it to a rare adverse reaction to, of all things, castor oil. So I'm thinking castor beans. Not the case. It's *ricin,* Lindsay! Relatively easy to make in large quantities. Protein derived from the castor plant."

"Obviously, it's poisonous, right?"

"*Highly* toxic. A couple of thousand times more powerful than cyanide," Claire said, nodding. "Easily secreted. A pinprick would stop your heart. It can also be released into the air, Lindsay. But I was thinking ricin alone wouldn't leave someone looking like that, unless it was delivered . . ."

"Unless it was delivered how?"

"Unless it was delivered in such massive amounts that it accelerated the destructive cycle by a factor of ten . . . fifty, Lindsay. This Bengosian, he was dead before the champagne glass fell. Ricin kills over a period of hours, even a day. You get severe, flulike warnings, gastrointestinal pains; your lungs fill up with fluid. This guy came back at eleven-thirty and they were calling it in by three o'clock. Three o'clock."

"We found a champagne glass shattered on the floor. We sent it to the lab. They can test for this stuff, right?"

"Testing for the stuff isn't what concerns me, Lindsay. Why kill him like this, when a *tenth* of this dosage would've done the trick?"

I saw where Claire was going. Whoever killed them had studied both victims. Both murders had been planned, set up. And the killer possessed weapons of widespread terror.

We are inside your homes, your work-places . . . They were telling us, We have this stuff. We can deliver ricin in massive quantities if we want to. "Jesus, they're warning us, Claire. They're declaring war."

Chapter 28

We called in everyone now. The Metropolitan Medical Task Force. The Bureau of Public Safety. The local office of the FBI. We weren't talking murder any longer. This was terrorism.

The trail for the missing au pair had gone cold. Jacobi and Cappy had come back empty after passing her photo around the campus bars across the bay. One thing did pan out, though: the article Cindy put in the *Chronicle* on X/L. With news crews plastered all over their offices and the threat of a sub-poena, I got a message from Chuck Zinn that he wanted to deal. An hour later, he was in my office.

"You can have your access, Lieutenant. In fact, I'll save you the trouble. Mort did receive a series of e-mails in the past few weeks. The entire board did. None of us took them very seriously, but we put our internal security team on it."

Zinn unbuckled his fancy leather case and placed an orange file on the table and pushed it across. "This is all of them, Lieutenant. By date received."

I opened the file and a shock resonated through my system.

To the Board of Directors, X/L Systems:

On February 15, Morton Lightower, your CEO, sold 762,000 shares of his company stock totaling $3,175,000.

On that same day, some 256,000 of your own shareholders lost money, making their net return −87% in the past year.

35,341 children of the world died from starvation.

11,174 people in this country died from diseases that were deemed "preventable" with proper medical care.

That same Wednesday, 4,233,768 mothers brought babies into conditions of poverty and hopelessness across the world.

In the past 24 months, you have sold off almost $600,000,000 of your own company stock and purchased homes in Aspen and France, returning nothing to the world. We are demanding contributions to hunger and world health organizations equal to any further sell-offs. We are demanding that the board of X/L, and the boards of all companies, see beyond the narrow scope of its expansionist strategies to the world beyond, which is being crushed by economic apartheid.

This is not a plea. This is a demand.

Enjoy your wealth, Mr. Lightower. Your little Caitlin is counting on you.

The message was signed, *August Spies*.

I skimmed through the rest of the e-mails. Each was more belligerent. The menu of the world's ills more grievous.

You're ignoring us, Mr. Lightower. The board has not complied. We intend to act. Your little Caitlin is counting on you.

"How could you not turn these over to us?" I stared at Zinn. "This whole thing might have been prevented."

"In retrospect, I understand how this must appear." The lawyer hung his head. "But companies receive threats all the time."

"This isn't just a threat." I tossed the e-mails back on my desk. "It's extortion, coercion. You're a lawyer, Zinn. The reference to his daughter is a blatant threat. You came in here to deal, Mr. Zinn. Here it is: This doesn't get out. The name on these e-mails stays between us. But we send in our own team to ascertain where they originated from."

"I understand." The lawyer nodded sheepishly, handing over the file.

I skimmed over the e-mail addresses. Footsy123@hotmail.com. Chip@freeworld. com. Both signed the same. *August Spies*. I turned to Jacobi. "What do you think, Warren? Can we trace these?"

"We already put them through our own investigation," Zinn volunteered.

"*You* traced them." I looked up, shocked.

"We're an e-traffic security company. All of them are free Internet providers. No user billing address. Nothing needed to open an account. You could go to the library, the airport, anywhere there's an open-access online terminal and open one yourself. This one was sent from a kiosk at the Oakland airport. This one from a Kinko's near Berkeley on University. These two, from the public library. They're untraceable."

I figured Zinn knew his stuff and was right, but one thing did jump out at me. The Kinko's, the library, the real Wendy Raymore's apartment.

"We may not know who they are, but we know *where* they are."

"The People's Republic of Berkeley," Jacobi said, and sniffed. "Well, I'll be."

Chapter 29

I stole away for a quick lunch with Cindy Thomas. Dim sum at the Long Life Noodle Company in Yerba Buena Gardens.

"You see the *Chronicle* this morning?" she asked, a pork dumpling sliding off her chopsticks as we sat on a ledge outside. "We lowered the boom on X/L."

"Thanks," I said. "I won't be needing you to run a follow-up."

"So, now it's your turn, right, to do a little rhythm for me."

"Cindy, I'm thinking this isn't going to be my case much longer, *especially* if anything leaks out to the press."

"At least tell me"—she looked at me solidly—"if I should be feeling these two murders are related?"

"What makes you think they're related?"

"Gee," she chortled, "two big-time businessmen murdered in the same city two days apart. Both of them ran companies on the wrong side of the headlines lately."

"Two totally different MOs." I held my ground.

"Oh? On one hand, we have a greedy corporate high roller sucking off tens of millions while his sales are going to rot; the other's hiding behind a bunch of high-priced lobbyists trying to screw poor people. Both are dead. Violently. What was the question, Linds? Why do I think they might be *related?*"

"Okay." I exhaled. "You know our arrangement? Absolutely nothing gets into print without my okay."

"Someone's targeting these people, aren't they?" She didn't mean the two already dead. I knew what she was saying.

I put the noodle container down. "Cindy, you keep your ear to the ground across the bay, don't you?"

"Berkeley? I guess. If you mean pitching in

with a couple of 'real-life success' pep talks in Journalism 403."

"I mean *under* the radar. People who're capable of causing trouble." I took in a breath and looked at her worriedly. "*This* kind of trouble."

"I know what you mean," she said. She paused, then shrugged. "There is stuff happening over there. We've all become so used to being part of the system, we forget what it's like to be on the other side. There are people who are growing . . . how should I put it . . . fed up. There are people whose message just isn't getting out."

"What kind of message?" I pressed.

"You wouldn't hear it. For God's sake, you're the police. You're a million miles away from these things, Lindsay. I'm not saying you don't have a social conscience. But what do you do when you read that twenty percent of the people don't have health insurance or that ten-year-old girls in Indonesia are pressed into stitching Nikes for a dollar a day. You turn the page, just like I do. Lindsay, you're gonna have to trust me if you want me to help."

"I'm going to give you a name," I said.

"This can't appear in print. You run it around on your own time. Anything you find, no copyeditors. No 'I have to protect my sources.' You come to me first. *Me, only.* Are we right on this?"

"We're right," Cindy said. "So give me the name already."

Chapter 30

"Beautiful," Malcolm whispered, his eyes narrowed through surgeon's operating lenses at the bomb on the kitchen table.

With still hands, he twisted the thin red and green wires that ran from the explosive brick into the terminal on the blasting cap and molded the soft, puttylike C-4 into the frame of the briefcase. "It's a shame to have to blow this up," he exclaimed, admiring his own work.

Michelle had come into the room and she placed a hand tremulously on Mal's shoulder. He knew this scared the shit out of her—wiring the thing, current and charges going everywhere.

"Relax, honey. No juice, no boost. It's the most stable thing in the world right now."

Julia was on the floor, listening to the TV, the auburn wig ditched after her assignment last night. There was a news interruption about the murder at the Clift. "Listen." She turned it up.

"While police are not yet linking Bengosian's death to Sunday's bombing at the home of a prominent Bay Area tycoon, sources say there is evidence to connect the two incidents, and they are looking for an attractive brunette female in her early to mid-twenties who was seen entering the hotel with George Bengosian."

Julia turned down the volume. "Attractive?" She grinned. "Honey, they will never know. Whatya think." She covered herself in the wig and struck a modeling pose.

Michelle pretended to laugh, but inside, she wished she hadn't been so stupid as to leave that goddamn inhaler lying around. She wasn't like Julia, who had killed a man last night looking right in his eyes. And now she was laughing about it, gloating.

"Mica, honey." Malcolm turned around. "I

need you to be a brave girl and place your finger on this spot." He taped the wired blasting cap to the soft C-4 and molded in the rigged cell phone. "This is the delicate part. I just need you to hold the green and red wires, baby, so they don't cross. . . . That would be very bad."

Mal always made fun of her. Just a Wisconsin cheesehead, he would say with a laugh. But she had proved herself. She put her finger on the wire, trying to show that she was brave. She wasn't a farm girl anymore.

"Nothing to get worried about." Malcolm winked, seeing her unease. "All that drama about crossing the wires, that's for the movies. Now what *is* certifiably hairy is that I set these little wires to the ringer, not the phone battery; otherwise, they'll be picking up our parts as far away as Eau St. Claire." Her hometown.

Michelle's finger was trembling. She didn't know if he was toying with her or not.

"Done." Malcolm finally exhaled, pushing the lenses up onto his brow. He wheeled back in the chair. "Juiced, as they say, and revved up to roar. Blow the dome right off of City Hall. Come to think of it, that's not a bad idea.

"Think we should take her out for a little test drive?" Mal said. "Whatya say?" Michelle hesitated. "C'mon," he said, grinning, "you look like you've seen a ghost."

He handed her a second cell phone. "Number's already punched in. Just remember, it's just a toy until the fourth ring. That's a no-no. You don't want to hear the fourth ring. Take the wheel, honey. . . . Let her rip."

Michelle shook her head and handed it back to him. Mal merely grinned.

"C'mon, nothing to worry about. No juice, no boost. It's all set up."

Michelle took a deep breath and pressed the SEND button, just to show she could. A second later, the phone wired to the bomb jangled.

"Contact." Malcolm winked.

A chill shot through her. Mal was so confident. He had it all planned. But things could go wrong. In the Middle East, Palestinian bombers blew themselves up all the time.

Beep. Her eyes went to the briefcase. Second ring. She tried to look calm, but her hand was shaking. "Malcolm, please." She tried to give it back. "You see it works. I don't like this, please. . . ."

"Please, *what,* Mica?" Malcolm held her wrist. "You don't trust me?"

The bomb phone jangled again. Third ring . . .

Michelle's blood went cold. "Cut it out, Mal." She fumbled for the disconnect button.

The next ring was contact. "Malcolm, please, you're scaring me."

Instead of complying, Mal pinned her hand. All of a sudden she didn't know what was going on. "Jesus, Mal, it's about to —"

Beep. Fourth ring.

The sound split the room like a scream. Michelle's gaze locked on the phone. On the bomb.

It began to vibrate. *Oh shit . . .* She looked into Malcolm's eyes.

A buzzer sounded.

No explosion. No flash. Just a sharp click. On the blasting cap.

Malcolm was grinning. He lifted the disengaged cap he'd been holding. "I told you, baby. No juice, no boost. So what'd you think? I think it drives just fine."

Michelle's body relaxed. Inside, she was screaming. She wanted to punch Malcolm in the face. But she was too spent. Sweat was pouring through her T-shirt.

Malcolm took the blasting cap and wheeled the chair back over to the device. "You think I was gonna set this beauty off?" He shook his head. "Fat chance, baby. She's got important work to do. This bomb is going to blow the minds of everybody in San Francisco."

Chapter 31

About seven, I was back at my desk. My teams scattered all around the area, chasing the leads we had. Cindy had gotten me a copy of this book, *Vampire Capitalism*. She said it would give me an idea of the new radicalism that was starting to take hold.

I flipped through the chapter headings: "The Failure of Capitalism." "Economic Apartheid." "Vampire Economics." "The Armageddon of Greed."

I didn't even notice Jill standing at my door. She knocked, making me jump. "If only

John Ashcroft could see you. The linchpin of the city's law-enforcement machine . . . *Vampire Capitalism?*"

"Required reading," I said, smiling, embarrassed, "for the serial killer with a bang."

She was dressed in a stylish red pantsuit and a Burberry summer raincoat, a pile of briefs squeezed into her leather satchel. "I figured you could use a drink."

"I could," I said, tapping the book against the desk, "but I'm still on duty." I offered her a bag of Szechuan soybeans instead.

"What are you doing," she snickered, "heading up the department's new Subversive Authors wing?"

"Very cute," I said. "Here's a fact I bet you didn't know. Bill Gates, Paul Allen, and Warren Buffet made more money last year than the thirty poorest countries, a quarter of the world's population."

Jill smiled. "It's good to see you developing a social consciousness, given your line of work."

"There's something bothering me, Jill. The fake secondary device outside Lightower's town house. The note on the company form balled up in Bengosian's mouth. These people have made their motive clear. But they're trying to taunt us. Why play the game?"

She balanced a red shoe on the edge of my desk. "I don't know. You're the one who catches 'em, honey. I just put 'em away."

There was a bit of a pause. A stiff one. "You mind if I change the subject?"

"Your soybeans," she said with a shrug, popping one in her mouth.

"I don't know if this'll sound silly. I was a little worried the other day. Sunday. After we ran. Those marks, Jill. On your arms. Something got me thinking."

"Thinking about what?" she asked.

I looked into her eyes. "I know you didn't get those marks from a shower door. I know what it's like, Jill, when you have to admit you're human, like the rest of us. I know how you wanted that baby. Then your dad died. I know you pretend that you can work everything out. But maybe you can't sometimes. You won't talk about it with anyone, even us. So the answer is, I don't know about those marks. You tell me."

There was a stubbornness in her eyes that suddenly turned fragile, something about to give. I didn't know if I had gone too far, but to hell with it, she was my friend. All I wanted was for her to be happy.

"Maybe you're right about one thing," Jill finally said. "Maybe those marks *didn't* come from a shower door."

Chapter 32

There are crimes that are brutal and inex-
cusable. Sometimes they make me sick, but
their motives are open. Now and then, I even
understand. Then there are the hidden
crimes. The ones you are never meant to
see. The kind of cruelty that barely breaks
the skin but crushes what's inside, the little
voice that is human in all of us.

These are the ones that really make me
wonder about what I do for a living.

After Jill told me what had been going on
between her and Steve, after I wiped her
tears and cried with her like a little sister, I

drove home in a daze. A pall had clung to her face, a whitewash of shame I will never forget. *Jill, my Jill.*

My first instinct was to drive over there that night and slap a charge on Steve. All along, the slick, self-righteous prick had been bullying her, hitting her.

All I could think of was Jill, the face I saw on her, that of a little girl. Not the Chief Assistant D.A., top of her class at Stanford, who seemed to breeze through life. Who put murderers away with that icy stare. My friend.

I tossed and turned the whole night. The following morning, it took all I had to focus on the case. Overnight the lab tests confirmed Claire's findings. It was ricin that had been ingested by George Bengosian.

I had never seen the Hall as tense as it was that morning, bustling with dark-suited Feds and media managers. I felt as if I was sneaking past security just to call Cindy and Claire.

"I need to see you guys," I told them. "It's important. I'll meet you at Susie's at noon."

By the time I arrived at the quiet counter café down Bryant, Cindy and Claire were squeezed into a corner booth. Both wore anxious looks.

"Where's Jill?" asked Cindy. "We figured she was coming with you."

"I didn't ask her," I said. I sat in the seat across from them. "This is *about* Jill."

"Okay . . ." Claire nodded, confused.

Piece by piece, I took them through my first suspicions about the marks I had seen on Jill while we were jogging. How I didn't like the looks of them and how maybe, in the aftermath of losing the baby, she had done them to herself.

"That's ancient history," Cindy shot in. "Isn't it?"

"You asked her?" asked Claire. Her gaze was deadly serious.

I nodded, my gaze fixed on hers.

"And . . . ?"

"She said, 'What if I didn't make those marks myself?'"

I watched Claire studying me, trying to read my face. Cindy blinking, beginning to understand.

"Oh, Jesus," muttered Claire. "For God's sake, you don't mean Steve . . ."

I nodded, swallowed.

A deep, sickening silence fell over the table. The waitress came. We ordered numbly. When the waitress left, I met their eyes.

"That son of a bitch." Cindy shook her head. "I'd like to cut off his balls."

"Join the club," I shot back, "that's all I thought about last night."

"How long?" asked Claire. "How long has this been going on?"

"I don't really know. She keeps saying it was the baby. When she lost it, Mr. Sensitivity there laid the blame on her. 'You couldn't do it, could you? The big hotshot. You couldn't even do what every other woman can. Have a child.'"

"We have to help her," Cindy said.

I sighed. "Any ideas how?"

"Get her the hell out," Claire said. "She can stay with one of us. Does she *want* out?"

I didn't know. "I'm not sure she's gotten there yet. I think what she's dealing with now is just shame. Like she's letting people down. Us. Maybe him. Strange as it sounds, I think there's a side of her that wants to prove she can be the wife, and mother, he wants her to be."

Claire nodded. "So we talk to her, right? When?"

"Tonight," I answered.

I looked at Claire. "Tonight," she agreed.

Our food came and we picked at it without much appetite. No one had even asked about the case. Suddenly Claire shook her head. "Like you didn't have enough going on."

"Speaking of which" — Cindy pulled up her bag — "I have something for you." She brought out a spiral notebook and ripped off a page.

Roger Lemouz. Dwinelle Hall. 555-0124.

"This guy's at Berkeley. In the Linguistics Department. Globalization expert. Be prepared: his view of life, let's just say, may not exactly coincide with yours."

"Thanks. Where'd you get this?" I folded the paper in my purse.

"I told you," Cindy said, "a million miles away."

Chapter 33

I pushed the situation with Jill to the back of my mind as best I could; I phoned and managed to catch Roger Lemouz in his office. We spoke briefly and he agreed to see me.

Just getting out of the Hall was a breath of fresh air. These days, I rarely went over to this part of the bay. I parked my Explorer near the stadium off of Telegraph Avenue and headed past the street rats hawking pot and bumper stickers. The sun was beating onto Sproul Plaza, students in backpacks and sandals sitting around, reading on the steps.

Lemouz's office was in Dwinelle Hall, an

official-looking concrete structure just off the main quad. "Please, it's open," a strong, Mediterranean accent answered my knock. A hint of something more formal, educated. British?

Professor Lemouz leaned back behind a chaotic desk in the small office cluttered with books and papers. He was large-shouldered and swarthy, with curly black hair falling over his forehead, a shadowy growth on his face.

"Ah, Police Inspector Boxer," he said. "Please sit, be my guest. Sorry the surroundings are not so plush." The room was musty and smelled of books and smoke. An ashtray and a pack of unfiltered Rothmans were on the desk.

I lowered myself into a seat across from him and pulled out my pad. I handed him a card.

"Homicide," Lemouz read, bunching his lips, seemingly impressed. "So I suspect it's not some rogue etymological nuance that brings you here?"

"Perhaps another interest of yours," I said. "You're aware, of course, of the events going on across the bay?"

He sighed. "Yes. Even a man with his nose in his books most of the time brings it out

now and then. Tragic. Totally counterproduc-
tive. Fanon said, 'Violence is its own judge
and jury.' Yet, one cannot find it completely
surprising."

Lemouz's phony sympathy appealed to
me about as much as a dentist's drill. "You
mind telling me just what you mean by that,
Mr. Lemouz?"

"Of course, Madam Inspector, if you would
be so kind as to tell me just why you are
here."

"It's *Lieutenant*," I corrected him. "I head
up the Homicide detail. And I was given your
name as someone who might have some
firsthand knowledge of what's going on here.
The ideological scene. People who might
find blowing up three sleeping people and
almost killing two innocent children as well
as virtually imploding someone's vascular
system an acceptable form of protest."

"By 'over here,' I assume you mean the
peaceful, academic groves of Berkeley,"
Lemouz said.

"By 'over here,' I mean *wherever* someone
would want to do these awful things, Mr.
Lemouz."

"*Professor*," he replied. "The Lance Hart

Professor of Romance Languages"—I saw the glimmer of a smile—"as long as we're spouting credentials."

"You said you didn't find these murders surprising."

"Why should they be?" Lemouz shrugged. "Should the patient be surprised he is ill when his body is covered in lesions? Our society is infected, Lieutenant, and the very people who transmit the disease look around and go, *'Who, me?'*

"Do you know," he said, raising his eyes, "that the powerful multinational corporations now have an output larger than the GNP of ninety percent of the countries around the globe? They have supplanted governments as the system of social responsibility in our world.

"Why is it," he laughed cynically, "we are so quick to rail against the moral outrage of apartheid when it threatens our racial sensibilities, but are so asleep to recognize it when it is economic. It is because we do not see it through the eyes of the subjugated. We see it through the culture of the powerful. The corporation. On TV."

"Excuse me," I interrupted, "but I'm here

about four gruesome murders. People are dying."

"Yes they are, Lieutenant. That's exactly my point."

There was a part of me that would like to have grabbed Lemouz by the lapels and shaken him. Instead, I pulled out the photo of the au pair on Wendy Raymore's ID and a police artist's sketch of the woman video-taped walking into the Clift Hotel with George Bengosian. "Do you know either of these women, Professor?"

Lemouz almost started to laugh. "Why would I want to help you? It's the state who is the architect of this injustice, not these two women. Please tell me, who has committed the larger injustice? The two women sus-pects"—he threw the front page of the *Chronicle* across the desk at me—"or these sparkling examples of our system?"

I was staring at photos of Lightower and Bengosian.

"If these people are signaling the start of a war," Lemouz laughed, "I say, let it unfold. What is the new phrase, Lieutenant?" He smiled. "The one Americans have embraced with all their moral imperative? *Let's roll.*"

I picked up the pictures, closed my pad,

and placed it back in my bag. I stood up, feeling tired and soiled. I walked out on the Lance Hart Professor of Romance Languages before I blew him up.

Chapter 34

I was steaming all the way back to the Hall thanks to Lemouz's sanctimonious rantings, plus my frustration that we weren't getting anywhere on these murders. I was still hot when I got to the office after six. I called Cindy and made a date to meet at Susie's. Maybe we could get *something* accomplished over lobster quesadillas. I needed the girls on this.

As I hung up with Cindy, Warren Jacobi stepped into my office. "Yank Sing," he said.

"Yank Sing?"

"It's a better bet than quesadillas. Dim sum. Women always open up with Chinese.

You should know that, LT. While you're there, they say the chicken in salt and ginger caused the downfall of the Qin dynasty.

"Where you been?" He sat down. He had something for me. I knew that sly grin of his.

"Out wasting my time, in the People's Republic. You got something, other than the restaurant review?"

"We got a hit on the Wendy Raymore APB," he said, grinning.

That got my juices flowing.

"A Safeway across the bay called in. Night clerk thought he recognized the face. There's a video on the way. He said she has red hair now and was wearing sunglasses. But she took them off for a second to count the cash, and he swears it's her."

"*Where* across the bay, Warren?"

"Harmon Avenue in Oakland." I drew a little mental map, and we both came to the same realization. "Near the McDonald's where little Caitlin was found."

Geographically, it was starting to fit into place. "Get that photo to every storefront in the neighborhood."

"Already done, LT." Jacobi's eyes had that little sparkle they got when he was holding something back.

"There been a lot of calls," I said, cocking my head at Warren. "What makes you think this one's real?"

He winked. "She was buying an asthma puffer."

Chapter 35

Cindy, Claire, and I had finished most of our Coronas and a plate of wings by the time Jill arrived. She hung her coat and came up warily to the booth, the nerves easy to read in her thin smile.

"So," she said, dumping her briefcase, and tossed herself next to Claire, "who wants to be first to prod?"

"No dissection," I said. "Wings . . . and here . . ." I tilted what was left of a beer into her glass.

We all raised our glasses, Jill a little hesitantly. We had this moment of quiet, everybody trying to figure out just what was right to say. How many times had we met together before? At first, four women with tough jobs who had come together just to pool our resources, solve a crime.

"To friends," Claire said. "Ones who will be there for one another. That means for anything, Jill."

"I'd better drink this," Jill said, her eyes starting to grow moist, "before I run my nose in it."

Jill drained about a third of the glass in a deep swallow. She drew a breath. "Okay, no reason to beat around the bush, right? You all know?"

Everyone nodded.

"Telephone, telegraph, tele-Boxer." Jill threw a wink my way.

"If you're in pain, we're all in pain," Claire said. "It would be the same for you if the roles were reversed."

"I know it would." Jill nodded. "So I guess what happens next is that you guys tell me I don't exactly fit the profile of the typical battered spouse."

"I think the only thing that's next," I said, wetting my lips, "is for you to tell us how you feel."

"Yeah." She drew a tight breath. "First, I'm

not battered. We fight. Steve's a bully. He's never hit me with a fist. He's never struck my face."

Cindy moved to object, but Claire held her back.

"I know that doesn't exonerate him, or justify anything. I just wanted you to know." She bit her bottom lip. "I guess I can't describe how I feel. I've tried enough of these cases to know the range of emotions. Mostly, I'm ashamed. I'm ashamed to admit that this is me."

"How long has it been going on?" Claire asked.

Jill leaned back and smiled. "You want the truthful answer to that question, or the one I've been telling myself the past few months? The truthful one is, from before we were married."

I felt myself clench my teeth.

"It was always something. What I would wear, something I would buy for the house that didn't fit his style. Steve's very big on telling me I'm stupid."

"Stupid?" Claire gasped. "You run intellectual rings around him."

"Steve's not dumb," Jill said. "He just doesn't see a lot of possibilities. At first, he would just squeeze me, like *here,* in the shoulders. Always pretend that it was inadvertent. Once or twice he threw things when he had a fit. My purse. Once, I remember"—she started to laugh—"it was this slab of Asiago cheese."

"Why?" Cindy shook her head, incredulous. "Why would he do these things to you?"

"Because I paid a bill late. Because I splurged on a pair of shoes when we were starting out and low on funds." She shrugged. "Because he could."

"This has been going on since we've known you?" I said, stunned.

Jill swallowed. "Guess I've been holding out on you guys, huh?" The waitress had brought some quesadillas and there was a Shania Twain song in the background. "It's like you're bribing me." She dipped a quesadilla in some guacamole and laughed. "New interrogation method. 'Yes, I know where Osama bin Laden is hiding, but please, another one of those little cheesy things if you would. . . .'"

We laughed. Jill always knew how to make us laugh.

"It's never the big things," Jill said. "It's always something trivial. The big things, I truly feel we really are partners in life. We've been through a lot together. But the small things . . . I accept a date for dinner with people he doesn't like. I forget to tell the housekeeper to take in his shirts. He makes me feel like I'm a stupid child. Ordinary."

"You're anything but ordinary," Claire said.

Jill dabbed at her eyes and smiled. "My cheerleaders . . . I could shoot the son of a bitch and you'd be praising my aim."

"We've already been discussing that option," Cindy said.

"You know I've actually thought about it." Jill shook her head. "About who would try my case. Hey, I think I've let things get a little melodramatic."

I asked, "How would you counsel a woman who came to you with the same predicament? Jill the prosecutor now. Not Jill the wife. What would you say?"

"I'd tell her I'd slap a suit on him so fast, it would be sticking to his ass the next time he took a shit," she said, and laughed.

One by one, we all laughed, too.

"You say you need a little more time," I said to Jill. "We're not here to make you change your life today. But I know you. You're staying around because you feel it's your responsibility to make this work. I want your promise, Jill. He doesn't even have to close his fist. If there's one more incident, I'll come and pack your things myself. My place, Claire's place, Cindy's . . . Well, forget Cindy's . . . it's a dump. But you've got choices, hon. I want you to promise, the next time he even *threatens* you, you're gone."

There was a sheen on Jill's face, a glimmer in those sharp blue eyes. Something made me think I had never seen her look prettier. Her bangs curled a little over her eyes.

"I promise," she finally said, blushing behind a smile.

"This is for real," Cindy pressed her.

Jill raised her palm. "The Highland Park Brownies, swear on your sister and never betray; otherwise, your face will break out with huge zits, oath."

"That sounds sufficient," Claire said.

Jill took our hands in the middle of the table. "I love you guys," she said.

"We love you, Jill."

"Now, can we goddamn order," she said. "I feel like I just took the law boards again. I'm starved."

Chapter 36

Maybe it was because I didn't sleep, tossing the whole night because this SOB—who was always the first to dash away when one of his buddies had the urge to go golfing, and pretended to be this fawning, adoring husband in public—was hurting one of the sharpest girls in the city, someone I loved.

Whatever it was, the thought of Steve gnawed at me for most of the next morning, until I could no longer sit there, fielding calls, pretending to keep my mind on the case.

I grabbed my purse. "If Tracchio's looking for me, tell him I'll be back in an hour."

Ten minutes later I pulled my car in front of 160 Beale, one of those glass skyscrapers off of lower Market filled with accountants and law partners, where Steve's office was.

All the way up to the thirty-second floor I was steaming, nearly hyperventilating. I pushed through the doors of Northstar Partnerships; a pretty receptionist behind a desk smiled at me.

"Steve Bernhardt," I said, dropping my shield in her face.

I didn't wait for her to call, but headed straight into the corner office I'd once visited with Jill. Steve was rocking back in his chair, in a lime green Lacoste shirt and khakis, on the phone. Without so much as breaking his tone, he winked and pointed me into a chair. *I got your wink, pal.*

I waited through the remainder of some business conversation, my anger growing as he peppered his call with overused tech clichés like "Sounds like you're trying to boil the ocean on that one, buddy."

Finally he signed off and spun around in his chair. "Lindsay," he said, eyeing me, as though he wasn't sure what was going on.

"Cut the crap, Steve, you know why I'm here."

"No, I don't." He shook his head, then sort of shifted his expression. "Is everything all right with Jill?"

"You know, I'm doing my best not to lunge across this desk and cram that phone right down your throat. Jill told us, Steve. *We know.*"

He shrugged, innocently, crossing a pair of Bass Weejuns in front of my face. "Know what?"

"I saw the bruises. Jill told us what's been going on."

"Oh"—he rocked back and arched his eyebrows—"Jill did say she was going out with the gang last night." He glanced at his watch. "Hey, I'd love to sit and take you through some of our personal shit, but I've got a twelve-thirty down the hall. . . ."

I leaned my face across the desk. "Listen to me. Listen closely. I'm here to tell you it stops. *Today.* You lay another hand on her . . . she breaks a nail that she doesn't want to discuss . . . she even comes into the office with a frown on her face, I'll get your name on an assault charge. You understand me, Steve?"

His expression never changed. He twirled the end of his short curly hair and chuckled,

"Gee, Lindsay, everyone always said you were a ballbuster, I just had no idea. . . . Jill has no right to bring you into this. I know this doesn't hold much weight with you full-time career types, with a dog and all . . . but we're in a marriage. Whatever goes on, it's between us."

"No longer." I glared at him. "Battery's a felony, Steve. I bust people like you."

"Jill would *never* testify against me," he said, then frowned. "Jeez, look at the time. . . . If you don't mind, Lindsay, they're expecting me down the hall."

I got up. I didn't know how he could act this way. We were talking about Jill. "I want to put this in a way you'll understand," I said. "You put one more mark on her, and the last thing you'll have to worry about will be Jill testifying. You go out for a run, you're in the garage late after work, you hear a noise that makes you jump . . . You'd *better* jump, Steve."

I went to the door, barely taking my eyes off of him. Steve sat there, rocking, some-where between speechless and inflamed. "Now, how's *that* for boiling the ocean, Steve?"

Chapter 37

Cindy Thomas sat at her desk at the *Chronicle,* not quite feeling herself. She twisted the cap on her Fruitopia organic apricot juice and took a sip. Then Cindy opened the paper and scanned the front page. One of her bylines was in the right-hand column. Bold headlines: SECOND CEO MURDER HAS POLICE RE-EXAMINING THE FIRST.

She flipped on her computer to check her e-mail. The hunk in the bulging tank top and construction belt who acted as her screen saver came to life. Cindy clicked Internet Explorer and her e-mail came up.

Twelve new.

She noticed one from Aaron, whom she had split with four months ago. *Having Pumpkinseed Smith at a recital at the church, 8:00 P.M., May 22. Can you make it?* Pumpkinseed Smith was one of the best horn players around! *You bet I'll make it,* Cindy typed back. *Even if it means I have to hear a sermon from you.*

She scrolled down the rest quickly. A response from a researcher who was doing background on Lightower and Bengosian. That bastard had been in court, fighting forty-six class actions from policyholders who were dumped in the past two years. What a sleaze!

She was about to delete the last message from an address she didn't know when the headline caught her eye. SLAM@ hotmail.com. It was titled, WHAT HAPPENS NEXT.

Cindy clicked on the message and prepared to send it to the ether grave of all spam. She took a swig of juice.

Don't ask how we got your name or why we're contacting you. If you want to do some good, you will do the right thing now.

Cindy rolled her chair closer to the screen.

The "tragic" incidents of the past week are only the tip of things to come.

The finance ministers of the world are meeting next week to carve up the last marginal remains of the "free" world economy left after Breton Woods—that which they have not already savagely consumed.

Cindy's heart was thumping as she read on.

We are prepared to kill one prominent blood-sucking pig every three days unless they come to their senses and denounce the global virus that is the system of free enterprise, that has imprisoned helpless nations in the Great Lie that trade will make them free; that has enslaved our fellow sisters into the sweatshop bondage of the multinationals, that has stolen the savings of the American worker in a stock market that is no more than a corrupt, insider scheme.

We are no longer isolated voices.

We are an army, just as lethal and far-reaching as the vampire superpowers.

Cindy blinked disbelievingly, almost unable to move. Was this some kind of Internet hoax? Somebody's idea of a joke?

She hit the PRINT key, clearing off her desk and cradling the phone in her neck as she read on.

The reason we have chosen you is that the normal channels of the media are as corrupt and self-serving as the global multinationals that own them. Are you part of the corruption? We'll soon see.

We ask the important people who will meet in San Francisco next week, the G-8, to do something historic. Unlock the chains. Forgive the debt. Stand up for freedom, not profit. Set back the machines of colonization. Open the economies of the world.

Until we hear that voice, you will hear ours. Every three days, another deserving pig will die.

You know what to do with this, Ms. Thomas. Do not waste your time trying to trace it. Unless you don't want to hear from us again.

Cindy's mouth was dry as dust. SLAM@hotmail.com. Was this real? Was someone messing with her?

She scrolled a little farther to the bottom of the page. For the next few seconds, she was unable to move.

The e-mail was signed, *August Spies.*

Chapter 38

Back at my desk, there was a message from Chief Tracchio waiting for me, and one from Jill.

"And the *Chronicle*'s waiting for you," my secretary Brenda called.

"The *Chronicle*?"

I looked up and saw Cindy, sitting knock-kneed on a stack of files outside my office. She pulled herself up as I approached, but I just didn't have the time for her.

"Cindy, I can't meet right now. I'm sorry. There's a briefing scheduled—"

"No," she cut in, stopping me, "I have

something to show you, Lindsay. This takes precedence."

"Is everything all right?"

She shook her head. "I don't think so."

We shut the door to my office behind us, and Cindy removed a piece of paper from her knapsack. It looked like e-mail.

"Sit down," she said. She put the page in front of me and sat next to me. "Read."

One look at Cindy's eyes and I knew this wasn't good.

"It came in my morning e-mail," she explained. "I'm listed on the *Chronicle* website. I don't know who it's from. Or why they sent it to me. It's just that I'm a little freaked right now."

I started to read. *Don't ask how we got your name or why we're contacting you. . . .* The more I read, the worse it got. *We are prepared to kill one prominent bloodsucking pig every three days. . . .* I looked up.

"Keep reading," Cindy said.

I looked back down and read the rest of the page. I was trying to decide if it was real. I reached the bottom, and knew that it was.

August Spies.

My chest was building up pressure. Suddenly, it was clear where all this was headed. They were holding the city hostage. This was a statement of terror. The G-8. Their target. It was scheduled for the tenth — in nine days. The finance ministers of the top industrial states around the world would be in San Francisco.

"Who knows about this?" I asked.

"You and me," Cindy said. "And them."

"They want you to publish their demands," I said. "They want to use the *Chronicle* as a soapbox." I was thinking of all the possible scenarios. "This is gonna make Tracchio shit."

The countdown had already started. *Every three days.* Today was Thursday. I knew this e-mail had to be turned over. And once I did, I knew it would no longer be my case. But there was something I needed to do first.

"We can try and trace the address," Cindy said. "I know a hacker—"

"It won't lead anywhere," I said. *"Think,"* I pressed her. "Why did they contact you? There are plenty of other reporters at the *Chronicle*. There's got to be a good reason."

"Maybe because my byline's on the story. Maybe because I have roots in Berkeley. But that was ten years ago, Lindsay."

"Could it be someone from back then? Someone you knew? That asshole Lemouz?"

We looked at each other. "What do you want me to do?" Cindy finally asked.

"I don't know. . . ." They had made contact. I knew killers enough to know that when they want a dialogue with you, when there's anything you can do to put off the next grisly act, you talk.

"I think I want you to answer it," I said.

Chapter 39

Everything seemed to be pointing to across the bay. The sources of the Internet messages. Where the Lightower baby was found. Lemouz. Wendy Raymore's pilfered ID. The clock was ticking. A new victim every three days . . .

I was tired of waiting for things to come to me. A swarm of FBI agents had descended on the Hall, tracing, dissecting, analyzing Cindy's message. It was time to take it to them, whoever was responsible for these outrageous murders.

Jacobi and I called on Joe Santos and

Phil Martelli, two Berkeley cops who headed up the Street Intel Unit. Santos had been around since the sixties — Robbery, Homicide, one of those old-line veterans who had seen it all. Martelli was younger, out of Narcotics.

"Basically, you've got every shitbag outfit going operating in the Free Republic," Santos said with a shrug. He popped a Mento. "You got your BLA, IRA, Arabs, free speech, free trade. Everybody with an axe to grind — and an axe — is over here."

"Word is," Martelli added, "we got some nasty riffraff from Seattle drifting down here to make some mayhem for the G-8 meeting, all those big economic geniuses, those world-beaters."

I brought out the case file, grisly photos of the Lightower town house and Bengosian. "We're not looking for a bunch of sign wavers, Phil."

Martelli smiled at Santos. He got it. "Other day," he said, "we got this undercover outfit staking out some SOB who's been creating a nuisance about PG and E." Pacific Gas and Electric. Our utility robber barons. Since Enron, there wasn't a person in California who didn't feel he wasn't being ripped off, and he was probably right.

"Everybody's got a grudge against those bastards," Jacobi said, "including me."

"This individual's doing a bit more than some casual bitching at the customer service rep. He's been picketing headquarters, handing out leaflets urging people not to pay their bill. Free People's Power Initiative, it was called. We got the sense," Santos said, chuckling, "that this was a *very* angry individual."

Martelli picked up the story. "Crazy bastard is always lugging around this big duffel. We figured it was filled with these leaflets of his. One day this undercover guy stops him and gets him to open the bag. Guy's got a goddamn M49 rocket launcher in there. Next we raid his house. There're grenades, C-4, blasting caps. The Free People's Power Initiative. They were planning to blow up the fucking power company over their bill."

"So, Joe," I said, shifting the subject, "you mentioned radicals moving down here to disrupt this G-8 meeting? That's a place to start."

"Do better than *that* . . ." Santos popped another Mento and shrugged. "One of our undercovers told us there's some kind of rally planned today. A B of A branch, over on Shattuck. Said some of the biggies'll be around. Why don't you come see for yourself. Welcome to our nightmare."

Chapter 40

Twenty minutes later, we pulled up about two blocks from the Bank of America location in Santos and Morelli's unmarked car. About a hundred demonstrators were crowded around the entrance to the branch; most were holding crudely painted signs: A FREE MONEY SUPPLY IS THE SIGN OF A FREE PEOPLE, one read. Another, GIVE THE WTO AIDS.

An organizer in a T-shirt and torn jeans was standing on the roof of a black SUV, shouting into a microphone, "Bank of America enslaves girls before puberty into oppression. Bank of America sucks the people's blood!"

"What the hell are these people protesting," Jacobi asked, *"mortgages?"*

"Who knows," replied Santos. "Child labor in Guatemala, the WTO, big business, the fucking ozone layer. Half of them are probably losers they pick off the welfare line and buy with a pack of smokes. It's the leaders I'm interested in."

He took out a camera and started snapping shots of people in the crowd. A ring of about ten police stood between the bank and the protesters, riot clubs dangling at their sides.

Things Cindy had said began to resonate. How in the comfort of your own life, you could just turn the page when you read about the uninsured or the poor, or underdeveloped countries drowning in debt. But how some people *couldn't* turn the page. A million miles away, right? Didn't seem like that now.

Suddenly a new speaker climbed on top of the SUV. My eyes bulged. It was Lemouz. Imagine that.

The professor took the microphone and began shouting. "What comprises the World Bank? It is a group of sixteen member institutions from all parts of the world. One of them is the Bank of America. Who loaned the money to Morton Lightower? Who were the underwriters who handled his company's IPO? The good old B of A, my friends!"

Suddenly the mood of the crowd changed. "These bastards *should* be blown up!" a woman shouted. A student tried to start a chant: "B of A. B of A. How many girls have you killed today?"

I saw pockets of violence begin to break out. A kid hurled a bottle at the window of the bank. At first I thought it was a Molotov, but there was no explosion.

"See what we have to deal with over here," Santos said. "Problem is, they're not all wrong."

"Fuck they're not," contributed Jacobi.

Two police officers invaded the ranks and tried to corral the bottle thrower, but the crowd banded together, impeding their way. I saw the kid take off down the street. Then there was screaming, people on the ground. I couldn't even tell where it all had started.

"Oh fuck." Santos put down his camera. "This could be getting out of hand."

One of the cops swung his stick and a long-haired kid sank to his knees. More people began to throw things. Bottles, rocks. Two of the agitators started wrestling with the police, who dragged them down, pinning them with their sticks.

Lemouz was still barking into the microphone. "See what the state must resort to — cracking heads of mothers and children."

I had taken about as much as I could sit back and watch. "These guys need help," I said, and went to open the door.

Martelli held me back. "We go in, we get made."

"I'm already made," I said, unstrapping the gun from my leg. Then I ran across the street with Martelli a few strides behind.

Cops were being shoved and pelted with debris. "Pigs! Nazis!"

I pushed my way into the throng. A woman held a cloth to her bleeding head. Another carried a baby, crying, out of harm's way. Thank God somebody had a little common sense.

Professor Lemouz's gaze fixed on me. "Look how the police treat the innocent voice of protest! They come with drawn guns!

"Ah, Madam Lieutenant," he said, grinning down from his makeshift podium, "still trying to get yourself educated, I see. Tell me, what did you learn today?"

"You planned this," I said, wanting to run

him in for disorderly conduct. "It was a peaceful demonstration. You stirred them up."

"A shame, isn't it? Peaceful demonstrations never seem to make the news. But look . . ." He pointed toward a news van pulling up down the street. A reporter jumped out, and a cameraman was filming as he ran.

"I'm watching *you,* Lemouz."

"You flatter me, Lieutenant. I'm just a humble professor of an arcane subject not in vogue these days. Really, we should have a drink together. I'd like that. But if you'll excuse me, there's a case of police brutality waiting for me now."

He bowed, produced a supercilious grin that made my skin crawl, then started to wave his arms over his head, stirring up the crowd, chanting, "B of A. B of A. How many girls have you enslaved today?"

Chapter 41

Charles Danko stepped into the depressingly drab lobby of the large municipal building. There was a security station to his left, two desultory guards inspecting bags and packages. His fingers tightened around the handle of the leather case.

Of course, Danko wasn't his name right now. It was Jeffrey Stanzer. Before that, it had been Michael O'Hara. And Daniel Browne. He had gone through so many names over the years, changing them, moving on whenever he felt people getting too close. Names were fungible, anyway — as easy to change as making a new driver's license. What had remained constant was a belief that burned deeply inside his soul. That he was doing something here that was very important. That he owed it to people close to his heart, people who had died for a cause.

But the scary thing—none of that was true.

Because Charles Danko believed in nothing but the hate burning inside of him.

He made a check of the security officers going about their work, but it was nothing new. He had seen it many times before. He stepped up to the platform and started to empty his pockets. He'd done this so many times over the past few weeks that he might as well actually work in this building. *Case over there:* he mouthed the words before they were spoken.

"Case over there," the security guard said, clearing a spot on the screening table. He flipped open the top.

"Raining yet?" he asked Danko as he passed it through the X-ray scan.

Danko shook his head, his heart barely skipping a beat. Mal had built a masterpiece this time, the contents molded right into the lining. Besides, these drones wouldn't know how to find the bomb even if they knew what to look for.

Danko walked through the metal detector and a beeper went off. He patted his jacket up and down and seemed surprised when he took the bulging device out from one of his pockets.

"Cell phone," he said, smiling apologetically. "Don't even know it's on me until it rings."

"Mine only rings when it's for the kids," the genial guard said with a grin.

How easy it was. How asleep these people were. Even with all the warnings around them. Another guard pushed his case to the end of the platform. He was in. The so-called Hall of Justice.

He was going to blow it to bits! He'd kill everyone in here. Without regrets or remorse.

For a moment Danko just stood there, gazing at the oh-so-busy people rushing back and forth, reminded of his years of staying low, the quiet, trivial life that he was leaving behind. His palms began to sweat. In a few minutes they would know he could strike anywhere. At the epicenter of their power, the very heart of the investigation.

We will find you, no matter how large your house or powerful your lawyers. . . .

What he was carrying was enough to blow out an entire floor.

He stepped inside a crowded elevator and pushed the button for the third floor. It filled with people coming back from lunch. Cops, investigators from the D.A.'s office, pawns of the state. With their families and pets, watching the Giants on the tube, they probably felt they weren't responsible. But they were. Even the man who swept the floors. They were all responsible, and if they weren't, who cared?

"Excuse me," Danko said on three, squeezing himself out with two or three other people. Two uniformed cops passed him in the hallway. He didn't flinch. He even smiled at them. How easy it was. The home of the D.A., the chief of police, the investigation.

They had let him walk right in! Morons!

They wanted to show they had this whole G-8 thing under control. He would show them that they didn't have a clue.

Danko took a breath and came to a stop in front of Room 350. HOMICIDE, it said.

He stood there for a moment, looking as if

he belonged. But then he turned and walked back to the elevator.

Dry run, he thought as he took the next car down.

Practice makes perfect. Then . . .

Boom! Yours truly, August Spies.

Part Three

Chapter 42

It was four by the time I left Berkeley and made it back to the office. My secretary, Brenda, happened to catch me in the hallway. "You've got two messages from A.D.A. Bernhardt, but don't get comfortable. The boss is asking for you upstairs."

As I knocked on Tracchio's door, a meeting of the Emergency Task Force was already under way. I wasn't surprised to see Tom Roach, from the local FBI. They'd been all over things since Cindy got the e-mail that morning. Plus Gabe Carr, the deputy mayor in charge of police affairs, and Steve Fiori, the press liaison.

And someone with his back to me whom I *didn't* recognize: dark, with thick brown hair, solidly built. The guy had advance team for the G-8 meeting stamped all over him. *Here we go, antacid lovers.*

I nodded to the guys I had worked with, a quick glance toward the suit I didn't know. "You want to bring everyone up to date, Lieutenant?" the Chief said.

"Sure," I said, nodding. My stomach churned. I hadn't exactly prepped for a presentation. I had the feeling I was being set up, Tracchio-style.

"A lot of things are pointing toward Berkeley," I explained. I ran off the key angles we were working. Wendy Raymore, the demonstration today, Lemouz.

"You think this guy's involved?" Tracchio asked. "He's a professor, right?"

"I ran his name and it came back with nothing deeper than a couple of unlawful demonstrations and resisting arrests," I said. "Both dropped. He's harmless. Or he's very, very smart."

"Any trace on the taggants in the C-4?" Tracchio asked. It felt as if he was trying to make points with the Fed in the tan suit. Who the heck was he anyway?

"It's with ATF," I said.

"And these people keep communicating on these public e-mail ports to threaten us," he said.

"What do you want us to do, stake out every public-access computer in the Bay Area?" I asked. "You know how many we're talking, Chief?"

"Two thousand one hundred and seventy-nine," the Fed in the suit suddenly chimed in. He flipped a sheet of paper. "Two thousand one hundred and seventy-nine public-access Internet access portals in the Bay Area, depending on how they're defined. Colleges, libraries, cafés, airports. That includes two in army recruiting centers in San Jose, but I don't think they'll try there, if that narrows it down at all."

"Yeah," I said as our eyes finally met, "that starts to narrow it down."

"Sorry." The man rubbed his temples and relaxed into a tired smile. "I just got off a plane from Madrid twenty minutes ago, expecting to check through some security details for the G-8 next week. Now I'm wondering if I suddenly find myself in the middle of the Third World War."

"Lindsay Boxer," I said.

"I know who you are," the Fed replied. "You worked that La Salle Heights church bombing last year. People in Justice took note. Any chance we can contain these people in the next week?"

"Contain?" The word had a Clancy-esque sound to it.

"Let's not play games, Lieutenant. We have a meeting of the heads of finance of the Free World coming here. Plus a threat to the public safety, and like the Chief said, we don't have much time."

There was a directness about this guy I liked. Not the usual Washington type.

"So everything's still on?" Gabe Carr, the mayor's deputy, asked.

"On?" The Washington man looked around the room. "The locations are secure, right? We have adequate manpower, don't we, Chief?"

"Every uniformed man on the force at your disposal next week." Tracchio's eyes lit up.

I cleared my throat. "What about the e-mail we received? What do we do with it?"

"What do *you* want to do with it, Inspector?" the Washington guy asked.

My throat was dry. "I want to answer it," I said. "I want to start a dialogue. Map out the contact points they respond from. See if they divulge something. The more we talk, the more they might reveal. . . ."

There was one of those sticky, protracted silences, and I was hoping I wasn't about to be shoved off this case.

"Right answer." The federal agent winked at me. "No need for all the melodrama, I just wanted to see who I was working with. Joe Molinari," he said, smiling, and pushed across his card.

As I read it, as hard as I tried not to change my expression, my heart picked up a beat, maybe a couple of beats.

DEPARTMENT OF HOMELAND SECURITY, the card read. JOSEPH P. MOLINARI. DEPUTY DIRECTOR.

Shit, this guy was all the way up!

"Let's start a dialogue with these bastards," said the deputy director.

Chapter 43

My head was still buzzing from my meeting with Molinari as I headed back to my office. On the way, I stopped at Jill's.

A worker was vacuuming the corridor, but her lights were still on.

An Eva Cassidy CD was playing lightly in the background. I heard Jill dictating into a recording device.

"Hey." I knocked on the door. A look as apologetic as I could muster. "I know you left some messages. It probably won't help if I tell you about my day."

"Well, I know how it *began*," Jill said. Icicles.

Deserved.

"Look, I can't blame you for being mad." I stepped in, placing my hands on the top of a high-backed chair.

"You could say I was a little mad," Jill said, "earlier in the day."

"And now?"

"Now . . . I guess you could call it *very* fucking mad, Lindsay."

There wasn't a hint of humor in her face. When you needed someone to seriously bust some balls—to use the wrong metaphor—Jill was your gal.

"You're torturing me," I said, and sat in the chair. "I realize what I did was way out of bounds."

Jill laughed derisively. "I would say the part about sending a hit man after my husband seemed a bit wide of the lines—even for you, Lindsay."

"It wasn't a hit man," I corrected her. "It was a knee-cracker. But who's being technical. What can I say? You're married to a total SOB." I pulled the chair up to the side of her desk. "Look, Jill, I know it was wrong. I didn't go there to threaten him. I went for you. But the guy was such a tight-assed creep."

"Maybe what *the guy* didn't appreciate

was our business being laid out like a laundry list in his face. What I told you was in confidence, Lindsay."

"You're right." I swallowed. "I'm sorry."

Gradually, the little lines of anger in her brow began to soften. She pushed back her chair from the desk and rolled it to face me, almost knee to knee.

"Look, Lindsay, I'm a big girl. Let me fight my own battles. You're my friend in this case, not the police."

"So everybody's telling me."

"Then hear it, honey, because I need you to be my friend. Not the 101st Airborne." She took my hands and squeezed them. "Usually a friend hears another out, invites her to lunch, maybe sets her up with a cute coworker. . . . Barging into her husband's office and threatening to have his knees capped . . . that sort of stuff . . . we call them *enemies,* Lindsay."

I laughed. For the first time I saw a glimmer of a smile crack through Jill's ice. A glimmer.

"Okay, so as a friend, how are you and the SOB since he punched you?" I sniffed back a false smile.

Jill laughed, shrugged. "I guess we're okay. . . . We talked about counseling."

"The only counseling Steve needs is from a lawyer, during an arraignment."

"Be my friend, Lindsay, remember. . . . Anyway, there are more important matters to discuss. What's going on in this city?"

I told her about the message Cindy had received that morning, and how it ratcheted up the case. "You ever hear of an anti-terrorism guy named Joe Molinari?"

Jill thought. "I remember a Joe Molinari who was a prosecutor back in New York. Top-notch investigator. Worked on the World Trade Center bombing. Not hard to look at, either. I think he went down to Washington in some capacity."

"'Some capacity' means the Department of Homeland Security *and* my new point man on the case."

"You could do worse," Jill said. "Did I mention he wasn't hard to look at?"

"Cut it out." I blushed.

Jill cocked her head. "Normally you don't go for the federal types."

"'Cause most of them are just career guys looking to score a promotion on our sources and leads. But this Molinari seems like the real deal. Maybe you could do some ground-work for me. . . ."

"You mean like what kind of litigator he is?" Jill smiled, cat-eyed. "Or whether he's married? I think Lindsay's a little taken with the special agent."

"Deputy director." I wrinkled my nose.

"Oh . . . the man's done well." Jill nodded approvingly. "I did say he was handsome, didn't I?" She grinned again. We both laughed.

After a while, I took Jill's hand. "I'm sorry I did what I did, Jill. It would kill me if I added to what you're going through. I can't promise to stay out, at least not completely. You're our friend, Jill, and we're worried sick for you. But I'll give you my word . . . I won't put a hit out on him. Not without running it by you first."

"Deal." Jill nodded. She squeezed my hand. "I know you're worried for me, Lindsay. And, really, I love you for it. Just let me see it through my way. And leave the cuffs at home next time."

"Deal." I smiled.

Chapter 44

For a Swiss, Gerd Propp had acquired a lot of American tastes and habits. One of them was going after salmon. In his room at the Governor Hotel in Portland, Gerd excitedly laid out on the double bed the new Ex Officio fishing vest he had just acquired, along with some hi-tech lures and a gaff hook.

His job, as an economist with the OECD out of Geneva, might be thought by some as stiff and tedious work, but it did bring him to the States several times a year and had introduced him to men who shared the same passion for coho and chinook.

And that was where Gerd was headed

tomorrow, under the guise of finalizing his speech before the G-8 gathering in San Francisco next week.

He put his arms through the brand-new fishing vest and regarded himself in the mirror. *I actually look like a professional!* As he adjusted his hat and puffed out his chest in his fancy vest, Gerd felt as energized and manly as a leading man in a Hollywood film.

There was a knock on the door. The valet, he assumed, since he had left word at the front desk to bring up a press for his suit.

When he opened the door, he was surprised to see a young man not in a hotel uniform at all but in a black fleece jacket and a cap hiding part of his face.

"Herr Propp?" the young man asked.

"Yes?" Gerd pushed his glasses up on his nose. "What is it?"

Before he could utter another word, Gerd saw an arm shoot toward him. It caught him in the throat, knocking the air out of him. Then he was shoved back onto the floor, landing hard.

Gerd tried to shake his head clear. His glasses were no longer on his face. He felt the ooze of blood running from his nose. "My God, what is going on?"

The young man stepped into the room and closed the door behind him. All of a sudden there was a dark metallic object in his hand. Gerd froze. His eyes were not too good, but there was no mistake. The intruder was holding a gun.

"You're Gerhard Propp?" the young man asked. "Chief economist of the OECD in Geneva? Don't try to deny it."

"Yes," Gerd muttered. "By what right do you barge in here and—"

"By the right of a hundred thousand children who die annually in Ethiopia," the man interrupted, "from diseases that could easily be prevented, if their debt repayments weren't *six times* their national health care coverage."

"Wh-what?" Gerd stammered.

"By the right of AIDS patients in Tanzania," the man went on, "who the government lets rot because they're too busy repaying the debt you and your well-heeled bastards have swamped them with."

"I'm just an economist," Gerd said. What did this man think he did?

"You are Gerhard Propp. Chief economist of the OECD, whose mission is to advance the rate by which the economically advantaged nations of the world expropriate the resources of the economically weak in order to convert them into the garbage of the rich." He took a pillow off the bed. "You are the architect of the MAI."

"You've got it completely wrong," Gerd said, panicked. "The agreements have brought these backward countries into the modern world. They have created jobs and an export market for nations that could have never hoped to compete."

"No, you are wrong!" the young man shouted at the top of his voice. He walked over and switched on the TV. "All it has brought is greed and poverty and plundering. And this TV bullshit."

CNN was on, the international business briefs, which seemed appropriate. Gerd's eyes bulged as he watched the intruder kneel down next to him, at the same time hearing the TV voice announce how the Brazilian real was under pressure again.

"What are you doing?" Gerd gasped. His eyes bugged out.

"I'm going to do what a thousand pregnant mothers with AIDS would like to do to you, Herr Doctor."

"Please," Gerd begged. "Please . . . you are making some kind of serious mistake."

The intruder smiled. He took a look at the supplies on the bed. "Ah, I see you like fishing. I can work with that."

Chapter 45

I got in to the office at seven-thirty the following morning and was surprised to find Deputy Director Molinari on the phone behind my desk. *Something* had happened.

He signaled for me to close the door. From what I could make out, he was talking with his office back East, getting briefed on a case. He had a stack of folders in his lap and he jotted down the occasional note. I could make out a couple: *9mm* and *Itinerary*.

"What's goin' on?" I asked when he hung up.

He motioned for me to sit down. "There's

been a killing in Portland. A Swiss national was shot in his hotel room. An economist. He was preparing to leave for Vancouver this morning on a fishing excursion."

Not to sound blasé, but we already had two national-security murder cases and the leaders of the Free World were eyeballing our every move. "I'm sorry," I said, "this relates to us, how?"

Molinari flipped open one of the folders he was holding, which turned out to be a set of crime photos he'd already had faxed from the scene. They showed a corpse in what looked to be a fishing vest with two bullet holes. His shirt was ripped open and his bare chest seemed to have had some letters scratched on it, *MAI.*

"The victim was an economist, Lieutenant," Molinari said, "for the OECD." He looked at me and smiled tightly. "That makes it clear."

As I sat down, my stomach sank. *Immediately clear.* Murder number three. I studied the crime shots more closely. Shots to the chest and a coup de grâce to the forehead. A large fisherman's hook in an evidence bag. The letters scratched into the victim's chest. *MAI.* "These letters mean anything to you?"

"Yeah," Molinari said, nodding. He got up. "I'll tell you about it on the plane."

Chapter 46

The "plane" Molinari had arranged for us was a Gulfstream G-3 with a red, white, and blue crest on the fuselage and the words GOVERNMENT OF THE UNITED STATES. The deputy director was definitely up there on the food chain.

It was my first time climbing aboard a private jet in the private section of SFI. As the doors closed behind us and the engines started up as soon as we hit our seats, I couldn't deny a thrill shooting through me. "This is definitely the way to travel," I said to Molinari. He didn't disagree with me.

The flight up to Portland was a little over

an hour. Molinari was on the phone for the first few minutes. When he got off, I wanted to talk.

I laid out the crime photos. "You were going to tell me what this meant. MAI?"

"The MAI was a secret trade agreement," he explained, "negotiated a few years back by the wealthy countries of the WTO. It extended to large corporations rights that sometimes superseded those of governments. Some people think it created an open hunting season on smaller economies. It was defeated in 1998 by a worldwide grass-roots campaign, but I'm told the OECD, which Propp worked for, was redrafting it and testing the waters again. Any ideas where?"

"The G-8 meeting next week?"

"Yeah . . . By the way" — he opened his briefcase — "I think you might get some use out of these." He handed me folders that turned out to be the intel jackets from Seattle I had requested. Each was stamped CONFIDENTIAL, PROPERTY OF THE FBI.

"Keep them close," the deputy director said with a wink. "Might prove a little embarrassing to me if they got out."

I skimmed through the records from Seattle. A few had prior records—everything from inciting a riot to resisting arrest and unlawful possession of a firearm. Others appeared to be students caught up in the cause. Robert Alan Rich had an Interpol file for inciting violence at the World Economic Forum meeting in Gstaad. Terri Ann Gates had been bagged for arson. A gaunt-faced Reed College dropout with tied-back hair named Stephen Hardaway had committed a bank robbery in Spokane.

"Remote-triggered bombs, ricin," I said, thinking aloud. "The technology is pretty advanced. Any of these connected enough to pull off the strikes?"

Molinari shrugged. "Somebody could've teamed up with an established terror cell. The technology's for sale. Or we could be dealing with a white rabbit."

"White rabbit? Like the Jefferson Airplane?"

"It's the name we give someone who's been hiding for a long time. Like the Weathermen from the sixties. Most of them have fit into society again. They have families, straight jobs. But there are a few still out there who haven't given up the cause."

A cabin door opened and the copilot said

that we were starting our descent. I stuffed the files in my briefcase, impressed with how quickly Molinari had followed up on my request.

"Any last questions?" he asked, tightening his seat belt. "There's usually a squadron of FBI officials who latch on to me when we land."

"Just one." I smiled. "How do you like to be addressed? Deputy director sounds like someone who runs a hydroelectric factory in the Ukraine."

He laughed. "In the field, generally 'sir' comes with the territory. But out of the field, what usually works for me is 'Joe.'"

He tossed me a smile. "That make it any easier for you, Lieutenant?"

"We'll see, *sir*."

Chapter 47

We were whisked by police escort from the private airfield outside Portland to the Governor Hotel in the center of town. The Governor was an old restored Western, and this was the worst thing that had ever happened there.

While Molinari conferred with the head of the regional FBI office, I got up to date with Hannah Wood, a local homicide inspector, and her partner, Rob Stone.

Molinari gave me time to go over the crime scene, which was definitely grisly. Clearly Propp had let his assailant in. The economist had been shot three times—

twice in the chest and a clean-through to the head, the bullet lodging in the floor. But Propp had also been slashed several times, probably with a serrated knife that still lay on the floor.

"Crime team dug this out." Hannah showed me a bag containing a flattened 9mm bullet. A large gaff hook in a Baggie was also being held for us.

"Prints?" I asked.

"Partials off the inside doorknob. Probably Propp's. The Swiss consulate's contacted Propp's family back home," Hannah said. "He had dinner with a friend scheduled last night, then a seven A.M. flight to Vancouver. Other than that, no calls or visitors."

I put on a pair of gloves, flipped open the briefcase on Propp's bed, and shuffled through his notes. A few books were scattered about, mostly academic stuff.

I went into the bathroom. Propp's toilet case was laid out on the counter. Not much else to go on. Nothing seemed to have been disturbed.

"Be easier if you could tell us what we're looking for, Lieutenant," Stone said.

I couldn't. The name August Spies hadn't been released yet. I focused on prints of the crime scene photos that were taped to the mirror. It was an ugly, horrible scene. Blood everywhere. Then the warning: MAI.

The murderers were doing their homework, I was thinking. They wanted a soapbox. They had it. So where the hell was the speech?

"Listen, Lieutenant," Hannah said uncomfortably, "it's not too hard to figure out what you and the deputy director are doing up here. That horrible stuff going on in San Francisco? This is connected, isn't it?"

Before I could answer, Molinari came in with Special Agent Thompson. "Seen enough?" he asked me.

"If there are no objections, sir"—the FBI man pulled out his cell phone—"I'll advise the anti-terror desk in Quantico that the killer is on the move."

"You okay with that, Lieutenant?" Molinari looked toward me.

I shook my head. "No. I don't think so."

The FBI man shot me a double take. "Run that by me again, Lieutenant?"

"I think you should wait." I gave weight to each word. "I don't think this murder is related to the others. I'm almost sure of it now."

Chapter 48

The room above might have just crashed through our ceiling, the way the FBI man blinked. To his credit, Molinari didn't react one way or the other. He seemed ready to hear what I had to say.

"You are aware of what Gerhard Propp did for a living? And why he was in this country in the first place?" Special Agent Thompson asked.

"I'm aware," I answered.

"And where he was scheduled to present next week?"

"I was briefed," I said. "Just like you were."

Thompson aimed a smug smile toward

Molinari. "So this is some *other* homicidal maniac who just happens to be targeting the G-8?"

"Yeah," I said. "That's exactly what I think."

Thompson laughed and flipped open his phone. He started to punch in his speed dial.

Molinari held his arm. "I'd like to hear what the lieutenant has to say."

"Okay . . . The first thing is, this crime scene is completely different from the others. One, this perp is probably male; that's clear from the force used to knock Propp to the ground. But that's not what I'm referring to. It's the physical condition of the body.

"The first two murders were detached." I pointed to the crime scene photo taped to the mirror. "This is emotional. Personal. Look at the cuts. The killer defaced the body. He used a handgun *and* a knife."

"You're saying there's a difference between blowing someone up, or pouring Drāno down their throat, and this?" Thompson said.

"Have you ever pulled a trigger on the job, Special Agent?"

He shrugged, but his face went red. "No . . . So?"

I took down the photo of Propp's body. "Could you do this?"

The FBI man seemed to hesitate.

"Different killers, different temperaments," Molinari cut in. "This one could be a sadistic maniac."

"All right, then there's the timing. The message yesterday indicated that there would be another victim every three days. That'd be Sunday. Too soon."

"More likely, the guy was available," the FBI man said. "You can't be saying you're holding a terrorist killer to his word?"

"I'm saying *precisely* that," I said. "I've been around pattern killers enough to understand them. There's a bond they make with us. If we can't take them at their word, why would we believe any of their messages? How would we confirm it's the same group behind their actions? They have to have total credibility."

Thompson looked to Molinari for help. Molinari's eyes were on me. "You've still got the floor, Lieutenant."

"The most important thing," I said, "there's no signature. Both San Francisco killings were signed. He wants us to know it's him. You almost have to admire the ingenuity. A knapsack posing as a secondary bomb left outside the town house. Bengosian's own business form stuffed in his mouth."

I shrugged at Molinari. "You can get every Ph.D. or forensic expert in the FBI or the National Security Council up here for all I care . . . but you brought *me* here. And I'm telling you, *this ain't him.*"

Chapter 49

"I'm ready to make that call." The FBI man nodded to Molinari, completely ignoring everything I'd just said. That really burned me.

"I just want to be clear, Lieutenant," Molinari said, focusing on me. "You think there's another killer, a copycat, at work here."

"It could be a copycat. It could be some sort of splinter group, too. Believe me, I wish I could say it was murder number three, because now we're left with a bigger problem."

"I don't understand." The deputy director finally blinked.

"If it isn't the same killer," I said, "then the terror has started to spread. I think that's exactly what's happened."

Molinari nodded slowly. "I'm going to advise the Bureau, Agent Thompson, to treat these cases as independent actions. At least for the time being."

Agent Thompson sighed.

"In the meantime, we still have a murder to solve. The man's dead here," the deputy director snapped. He looked around the room, his gaze ending up on Thompson. "Anyone have a problem with that?"

"No, sir," Thompson said, flipping his phone back into his jacket pocket.

I was stunned. Molinari had backed me up. Even Hannah Wood mooned her eyes in his direction.

We spent the rest of the day at the FBI regional office in Portland. We interviewed the person Propp was meeting in Vancouver and his economist friend at Portland State. Molinari also brought me in on two calls back to senior investigators at his home office in D.C., backing up my theory that this was a copycat crime and that the terror might be spreading.

About five, it dawned on me that I couldn't

stay up there much longer. There were a couple of fairly prominent cases that needed my attention back home. Brenda informed me there was a Southwest flight back to San Francisco at 6:30.

I knocked on the gray, carpet-covered cubicle Molinari was using for an office. "If you don't need me up here anymore, I thought I'd head home. It was fun being 'Fed for a Day.'"

Molinari smiled. "Look, I was hoping you might stay a couple of hours. Have dinner with me."

Standing there, I did my best to pretend that it didn't matter hearing those words, but my general rule about Feds notwithstanding, I was curious. Who wouldn't be?

But a few reasons why I *shouldn't* be popped into my head as well. Like the murder cases on my board. And the fact that Molinari was the second most powerful law-enforcement figure in the country. And unless I was misreading the little tingle bubbling up my spine, knocking down the old Chinese wall in the middle of a high-profile murder investigation wasn't exactly the best protocol.

"There's an eleven o'clock back to San

Francisco," Molinari said. "I promise I'll have you to the airport in plenty of time. C'mon, Lindsay."

When I hesitated one more time, he stood up. "Hey, if you can't trust Homeland Security . . . who can you trust?"

"Two conditions," I said.

"Okay," the deputy director agreed. "If I can."

"Seafood," I said.

Molinari showed the outline of a smile. "I think I know just the place. . . ."

"And no FBI agents."

Molinari's head went back in a laugh. "That's the one thing I can definitely guarantee."

Chapter 50

"Just the place" turned out to be a café called Catch, down on Vine Street, which was like Union Street back home, filled with trendy restaurants and cutesy boutiques. The maître d' led us to a quiet table way in the back.

Molinari asked if he could handle the wine, ordering a pinot noir from Oregon. He called himself a "closet foodie" and said what he missed most about a normal life was just staying home and puttering around the kitchen.

"Am I supposed to believe that one?" I grinned.

He laughed out loud. "Figured it was worth a try."

When the wine came I held up my glass. "Thank you. For backing me up today."

"Nothing to thank," Molinari said. "I felt you were right."

We ordered, then talked about everything but work. He liked sports—which was all right with me—but also music, history, old movies. I realized that I was laughing and listening, that time was going by pretty smoothly, and that for a few moments all of the horror seemed a million miles away.

Finally, he mentioned an ex-wife and a daughter back in New York.

"I thought all the deputy-level personnel had to have a little woman back home," I said.

"We were married fifteen years, divorced for four. Isabel stayed in New York when I started work in Washington. At first, it was just an assignment. Anyway"—he smiled wistfully—"like many things, I would do it differently if I could. How about you, Lindsay?"

"I was married once," I said. Then I found myself telling Molinari "my story." How I was married right out of school, divorced three years later. His fault? My fault? What difference did it make? "I was close again a couple of years ago. . . . But it didn't work out."

"Things happen," he said, sighing, "maybe for the best."

No," I said. "He died. On the job."

"Oh," Molinari said. I knew he was feeling a little awkward. Then he did a lovely thing. He simply put his hand on top of my forearm— nothing forward, nothing inappropriate—and squeezed gently. He took his hand away again.

"Truth is, I haven't been out much lately," I said, and lifted my eyes. Then trying to salvage the mood, I chuckled. "This is the best invitation I've had in a while."

"It is for me, too." Molinari smiled.

Suddenly his cell phone beeped. He reached in his pocket. "Sorry . . ."

Whoever it was seemed to be doing most of the talking. "Of course, of course, sir . . . ," Molinari kept repeating. *Even the deputy director had a boss.* Then he said, "I understand. I'll report back as soon as I have anything. Yes, sir. Thank you very much."

He flipped the phone back into his pocket. "Washington . . . ," he apologized.

"Washington, as in the *director* of homeland security?" It gave me a bit of a kick to see Molinari as part of a pecking order.

"No." He shook his head and took another bite of his fish. "Washington, as in the White House. That was the vice president of the United States. He's coming out here for the G-8."

Chapter 51

I can be wowed.

"If I wasn't a Homicide lieutenant," I said, "I might believe that line. The vice president just called you?"

"I might press *69 and show you," Molinari said. "Except that it's important we begin to establish more trust."

"Is that what we're doing tonight?" I asked, smiling in spite of myself.

Whatever was starting to happen, those little pinballs pattering inside were now crashing around my ribs like the drums in "Sunshine of Your Love." I was aware of the tiniest film of sweat at my hairline. My sweater was starting to feel prickly. Molinari reminded me of Chris.

"I hope we're starting to trust each other," he finally said. "Let's leave it at that for now, Lindsay."

"Aye-aye, sir," I said.

He paid the check, then helped me on with my jacket. I brushed against his arm and, well, electricity flared. I glanced at my watch. 9:30. Forty minutes to the airport to catch that flight I needed to be on.

Outside, we walked a block or two along Vine Street. I wasn't really paying attention to the shops. The night was cool but very pleasant. What was I doing here? What were the two of us doing?

"Lindsay"—he finally stopped to face me—"I don't want to say the wrong thing. . . ." I wasn't sure what I wanted him to say next. "My driver's down the block if you want. . . . But there's always the six A.M. flight."

"Listen . . ." I wanted to touch his arm, but I didn't. I'm not even sure why not.

"Joe," he said.

"Joe." I smiled. "Was this what you meant by being out of the field?"

He took my bag and said, "I was just thinking it'd be a shame to waste a perfectly good change of clothes."

I do trust him, I was thinking. Everything about Joe Molinari inspired trust. And I definitely liked him. But I still wasn't sure if this was a good idea, and that told me all I needed to know for right now.

"I think I'm just gonna let you think I'm a bit harder to get than I really am"—I bit my lip—"and make that flight at eleven."

"I understand. . . ." He nodded. "It doesn't feel right to you."

"It's not that it doesn't feel right." I touched his hand. "It's just that I didn't vote for your administration. . . ." Molinari laughed out loud. "But just for the record, it wasn't the wrong thing to say."

That made him smile, too. "It's getting late," he said. "I have some things to attend to up here. I'll be seeing you soon enough."

Then Molinari waved down the block for his car. The black Lincoln drove up. The driver climbed out and opened the door for me. Still not completely sure that I was doing the right thing, I got in.

Suddenly something hit me and I rolled down the window. "Hey, I don't even know what flight I'm on."

"Taken care of," Molinari said. He waved and slapped the side. The car started to pull away.

As soon as we were on the highway, I shut my eyes and began to review the day, but mostly my dinner with Molinari. After a while the driver said, "We're here, ma'am."

I looked outside and saw that we were at some remote part of the airfield. Yep, I can be wowed. Waiting for me on the tarmac was the Gulfstream G-3 jet I had flown up in that morning.

Chapter 52

Jill had it all planned out. And in her mind, it was going well.

She had come home early and prepared one of Steve's favorite meals, coq au vin. In truth, other than half a dozen kinds of eggs, it was the only thing she knew how to cook—or at least that she was confident about.

Maybe tonight they could talk about how to proceed. She had the name of a therapist that a friend had given her and Steve had promised he would actually go this time.

She had vegetables simmering in the pan and was about to add wine when Steve came home. But when he walked up the stairs, he seemed to look right through her. "Look at us," he said. "You'd think we were an ad for domestic bliss."

"Trying," Jill said. She was wearing pressed jeans and a pink V-necked T-shirt, and she had her hair down the way he liked it.

"Just one thing wrong." Steve tossed his newspaper down. "I'm going out."

Jill felt her stomach sink. "Why? Look at me, Steve. I've gone to a lot of trouble."

"Frank needs to bounce a proposal off me." Steve reached across to a fruit basket and took a peach. There was a part of him that seemed almost to be gloating, amused that he'd ruined the evening.

"Can't you see Frank at the office tomorrow? I told you, there was something I needed to talk about. You said okay. I've got all this food."

He took a bite out of the peach and laughed. "You break one night before eight and get it in your head to play Alice on *The Brady Bunch,* and *I'm* the one blowing the script?"

"It's not a script, Steve."

"You wanna talk"—he sucked out another bite of the peach—"go ahead. In case you've forgotten, it's still my check that pays for those Manolo Blahniks. The market the way it is these days, the only thing scarcer than the Ice Queen with an urge to have sex is a promising deal. Given the odds, I'll throw in with the deal."

"That was really cruel." Jill glared at him. She was determined to hold herself together. "I was trying to do something nice."

"It is nice." Steve shrugged, took another bite. "And if you hurry, you might still catch one of your girlfriends to share this special moment with you."

She saw herself reflected in the window, suddenly feeling ridiculous. "You're an incredible bastard."

"Aw . . ." Steve whined.

Jill flung the spatula down, grease splattering over the counter.

"That's a five-thousand-dollar slab of limestone you're redecorating there," Steve said.

"Goddamn you," Jill cried, her eyes starting to well up with tears. "Look what I'm trying to do for you." Everything had fallen apart. What was she trying to hold on to anyway?

"You belittle me. You criticize. You make me feel like crap. You want to walk out that door, *go.* . . . Get out of my life. Everyone thinks I'm crazy for wanting to keep this together anyway."

"*Everyone . . .*" She saw the venom in his eyes, the switch suddenly tripped. He grabbed her by the arm and squeezed it hard, forcing Jill down to the floor. "You let those bitches run your life. *I* run your life. *Me,* Jill . . ."

Jill held back more tears. "You're gone, Steve. It's over!"

"It's over when I say it's over," he said, hovering close to her face. "When I make your life so miserable, you beg me to leave. And I will, Jill. Until then, this is the way it is. It's not *over,* honeybuns. . . . Things are just starting to warm up."

"Get out," she said, and pulled away from him.

He cocked his fist, but she didn't even flinch. Not this time. Not even a blink. Steve moved fast, as though he was going to strike, and Jill just held her ground. "Get out, Steve," she seethed again.

The blood seemed to drain from Steve's face. "My pleasure," he said, backing away. He picked up another peach from the basket and rubbed it against his shirt. He tossed a last smirk toward the messy stove.

"Be sure and save the leftovers."

As soon as she heard the door close downstairs, Jill broke into tears. That was it! She didn't know if she should call Claire or Lindsay. There was something she had to do first. She pulled the Yellow Pages out of a kitchen cabinet and paged through them, frantically dialing the first number she found.

Her hand was trembling, but this time there was no turning back. *Answer, someone . . . please!*

"Thank God," she said when a voice finally did.

"Safe-More Locksmiths . . ."

"You do emergencies?" Jill asked, resolve mixed with her tears. "I need someone over here now."

Chapter 53

My message light was flashing.

It was after one in the morning when I finally got back to my apartment.

I threw my suit jacket over a chair and pulled off my sweater, hitting the PLAYBACK button of the answering machine.

5:28. Jamie, Martha's vet. She's ready to be picked up in the morning.

7:05. Jacobi, just checking in.

7:16. Jill. A quiver of nerves in her voice. "I need to talk to you, Lindsay. I tried your cell

phone, but it didn't answer. Call me, whenever you get home."

11:15. Jill again. "Lindsay? Call me as
soon as you get home. I'm up."

Something had happened. I punched in
her number and she answered on the second ring. "It's me. I was in Portland. Is everything okay?"

"I don't know," she said. A pause. "I threw
Steve out tonight."

I almost dropped the phone on the floor.
"You really did it?"

"This time's for keeps. We're done, Lindsay."

"Oh, Jill . . ." I thought of her carrying this
all night, waiting for me to come home.
"What did he do?"

"I don't want to go into it right now," she
said, "other than it won't be happening anymore. I threw him out, Lindsay. I changed the
locks."

"You locked him out? Wow! So where is he
now?"

Jill coughed out a laugh. "I don't have any
idea. He went out about seven and when he
came back, about eleven-thirty, I heard him

pounding on the door outside. It would have been worth the past ten years of bullshit just to see the expression on his face when his key didn't fit. He'll swing by tomorrow to get his stuff."

"Are you alone? Have you called anyone?"

"No," she answered. "I was waiting for you. My buddy."

"I'm gonna come over," I said.

"No," she said, "I just took something. I want to go to sleep. I have to be in court tomorrow."

"I'm proud of you, Jilly."

"I'm proud of me, too. You're not going to mind if I need a little hand-holding over the next few weeks?"

"No hand I'd rather hold. I'm giving you a big hug, honey. Get some sleep. And here's some advice from a cop: Keep that door locked."

I hung up the phone. It was going on two in the morning, but I didn't care. I wanted to call Claire or Cindy and tell them the news.

Jill finally booted the asshole out!

Chapter 54

"Hey, Lieutenant," Cappy Thomas shouted as I walked in the following morning. "Leeza Gibbons on the line. *Entertainment Tonight*? Wants to know if you can do lunch."

I had made the mistake of calling Jacobi from the plane last night, and maybe gave a few too many details about the day. Some snickers rippled around the squad room.

I took some hot water back to my desk. A light was flashing on my phone. I punched it in.

"Listen, LT"—Jacobi's voice—"me and the

missus were thinking about heading over to the Big Island sometime in July. Any chance you can snag the G-3?"

I punched off the line, spooning a pouch of Red Zinger into my mug.

"Hey, LT, *phone!*" Cappy yelled again.

This time I picked it up and snapped, "Look, I didn't sleep with him, I didn't ask for the jet, and while you bozos were scratching your balls back here, I actually moved the homicide case along."

"I guess that'll have to do as an update." Cindy laughed.

"Oh God . . ." I lowered my head, letting the blood drain from my face.

"Believe it or not, I didn't call to bust your chops. I've got news."

"I've got news, too," I said, thinking of Jill.

"Yours first." Cindy's tone was urgent, so I didn't think she was talking about Jill.

"Your fax should be ringing any second."

Just then Brenda knocked on my window, and handed me Cindy's transmittal.

Another e-mail.

"This was on my computer when I got to work this morning," Cindy said.

I was jolted back to reality. This time the

sending address was MarionDelgado@hot-mail.com.

The message was only one line: *That wasn't us in Portland.*

It was signed, *August Spies.*

Chapter 55

"I've got to take this upstairs," I said, shooting out of my chair, almost pulling the phone out of the wall. I was halfway up to Tracchio's office before I realized I forgot to tell Cindy about Jill. Things were going too fast now.

"He's behind closed doors," his secretary warned. "You'd better wait."

"This can't wait," I said, and pushed the door open. Tracchio was used to my barging in.

He was facing me, seated at his conference table. He was flanked by two others with their backs to me. One was Tom Roach, the local FBI liaison.

I almost fell when I saw that the other was Molinari.

I felt as if I had hit a wall, bouncing off and vibrating like in the Roadrunner cartoons.

"Soon enough, Lieutenant," Molinari said, rising.

"Yeah, that was what you said. I thought you had pressing matters in Portland."

"I did. They're taken care of now. And we have a killer to catch down here, don't we?"

Tracchio said, "We were just about to call you, Lindsay. The deputy director informed me how well you handled the situation up there in Portland."

"Which situation was he referring to?" A glance Molinari's way.

"The Propp homicide, of course." He motioned for me to sit down. "He said you were helpful in putting forth your theory of the crimes."

"Okay"—I handed Tracchio Cindy's e-mail—"then you should *love* this."

Tracchio scanned the page. He passed it across to Molinari.

"This was sent to the same reporter at the *Chronicle*?" he asked.

"Seems like they got a regular chat room going on," Molinari replied as he read. "We could make that useful." He pursed his lips. "I was just asking the Chief if you could work directly with us. We need help here on the ground. I'll need a place to work. I want to be right in the thick of it, Lieutenant. In your squad room if possible. That's how I work best."

Our eyes met. I knew we weren't playing games. It was a matter of national security.

"We'll find you an office, sir. In the thick of it."

Chapter 56

Molinari was waiting for me out in the hall, and as soon as Roach had ducked into the elevator, I looked at him reprovingly. *"Soon enough,* huh?"

He followed me down the stairwell to my office. "Look, I had the local FBI office to placate up there. There's always a lot of politics. You know that."

"Anyway, I'm glad you're here," I said, holding the stairwell door for him. I let it close. "I never had a chance to thank you for the ride. So, thanks."

I put Molinari in our squad room, cleared out a small office for him to work in. He told me he had declined something more fitting and private on the fifth floor next to the Chief.

It proved to be not such a bad thing, having the Department of Homeland Security working hand in hand with us, though Jacobi and Cappy looked at me as though I'd gone over to the enemy. Within two hours he had traced back the origin of the latest e-mail: an Internet café called the KGB Bar in Hayward that was popular with students across the bay.

And also who Marion Delgado was—the latest Hotmail address.

Molinari draped a fax from the FBI computers across my desk. An old newswire story, with a grainy photo of a grinning, gap-toothed kid in a peasant smock holding a brick in his hand. "Marion Delgado. He was some five-year-old who in 1967 derailed a freight train in Italy by tossing a brick in its path."

"Is there a reason you're thinking this is important to the investigation?" I asked.

"Marion Delgado was a rallying cry for revolutionaries in the sixties," Molinari said. "A five-year-old who stood up and stopped a train. The name became a code name to thwart undercover surveillance. The FBI was bugging phones like crazy, trying to infiltrate the Weathermen. They logged hundreds of messages from Marion Delgado."

"What are you saying—one of the old Weathermen is behind this current mess?"

"It wouldn't hurt to get the names of known members back then who haven't been brought in."

"That's a good idea," I said as I opened my desk and took out my gun. "In the meantime, you want to tag along while I go check out the KGB Bar?"

Chapter 57

In the long tradition of counterculture dives, where a cop walking in was about as welcome as an ACLU recruiter at a skinhead convention, the KGB set the bar at a new low. There were narrow rows of chipped pine tables with societal dropouts slouched in front of computer screens. Plus a mixed collection of riffraff sucking cigarette butts at the bar. Not much else caught my eye at first.

"You sure you're up for this?" I muttered to Molinari. "It'll be hard to explain if I got your face bashed in here."

"I was a prosecutor back in New York,"

Molinari said, and stepped forward. "I love this shit."

I went up to the bartender, a skinny mouse-faced guy in a muscle shirt with tattoos up and down both arms and a very long ponytail. After about fifteen seconds of being ignored, I leaned over and caught his eye. "We were just passing by and were wondering if anyone would like to support our fellowship mission in Chad?"

I couldn't get a half-smile out of him. He poured a beer for a black guy in an African skullcap seated two stools down.

"Okay, we're cops"—I dropped my shield—"you saw right through me."

"Sorry, we're a private club," the bartender said. "Need to see a membership card."

"Hey, just like Costco," I said, glancing at Molinari.

"Yeah, like Costco." The bartender grinned.

Molinari leaned forward, wrapping his hand over Ponytail's as he went to draw a beer. He put a silver shield with the words DEPARTMENT OF HOMELAND SECURITY in the guy's face. "I want you to follow this closely. I take my phone, and in about ten seconds a team of federal agents will barge in here and rip this place down to the two-by-fours. Now as I look around, there's probably about fifteen, twenty thousand dollars in computers in here, and you know how clumsy these police goons can be when they're lugging heavy evidence. So we need to ask you a few questions."

Ponytail glared at him.

"What do you say, Six-pack," the black man in the African skullcap spoke up, "under the circumstances I think we can waive the membership requirement this once."

He turned and faced us, a cheerful grin beneath the skullcap, saying in a deep British accent, "Amir Kamor. Six-pack was just expressing his desire to keep the clientele here on its usual high level. No need to make harsh threats. Please, can I invite you into my office?"

"*Six-pack?*" I glanced at the bartender and rolled my eyes. "That's creative."

In the rear there was a cramped private cubicle, barely larger than a desk. The walls were papered with posters and event notices—activist stuff, rallies for the poor, Free East Timor, AIDS in Africa.

I passed Amir Kamor my Homicide card and he nodded, as if impressed. "You said you have a few questions."

"Were you here last night, Mr. Kamor?" I started in. "Around ten P.M.?"

"I'm here every night, Lieutenant. You know the food and liquor business. It's all about whose hands are in the register."

"An e-mail was sent from here last night, at ten-oh-three P.M."

"Messages are sent from here every night. People use us as a source to air ideas. That's what we do here. Air ideas."

"You have a way of determining who was here? Anybody out of the ordinary?"

"Anyone who comes in this place is out of the ordinary." Kamor grinned. No one smiled at his joke. "Ten o'clock, you say . . . The place was filled. It may help if you could tell me just whom you're looking for or what they've done?"

I took out the photo of Wendy Raymore and the sketches of the woman who had accompanied George Bengosian. Kamor studied them, ridges digging into his wide brow. He sighed deeply. "I may have seen them over the years or I may have not. Our customers tend to come and go."

"Okay, then what about these?" I switched gears, taking out the FBI photos from Seattle. One by one, he leafed through them, merely shaking his head.

Then I noticed that he stared twice and blinked.

"You recognize someone. . . ."

"Merely a thought," he said, shaking his head. "I don't think so. Honestly."

"No, you recognized a face. Who was it?"

I re-laid the photos in a pattern on his desk.

"Remind me, Madam Lieutenant," Kamor said, looking up, "why do I want to assist the police on this? Your state is one that is built on corruption and greed. As the enforcers of its will, you are part of its foundation."

"I guess there's always *this,*" Molinari said. He put his face close to the startled Kamor's. "I don't really give a damn about what you jerk yourselves off about in here, but you should also know what security bill these crimes will be adjudicated under. We're not talking withholding evidence, Mr. Kamor. We're talking treason and conspiracy to commit terror. Take a look at the photos one more time. Please."

"Trust me, Mr. Kamor," I said, meeting his eyes, "you don't want to be anywhere near the heat on this one."

The veins on the bar owner's neck began to swell. He lowered his eyes and leafed through the photos again. "Maybe . . . I don't know . . . ," he muttered.

After some hesitation, he nudged one out. "He's different now. His hair is shorter, not so much like a hippie. He has a beard. He's been in here."

Stephen Hardaway. Alias Morgan Bloom. Alias Mal Caldwell.

"Is he a regular? How do we find him? This is important."

"I don't know." Kamor shook his head. "That is the truth. I remember him, once or twice some time ago. I think he came from somewhere up north.

"One more thing . . ." Kamor swallowed. "You will remember this the next time you barge in and threaten to deprive me of my rights."

He flicked another photo forward. Another face he knew.

"This one, I saw in here last night."

We were staring at Wendy Raymore, the au pair.

Chapter 58

We weren't back in the car for five seconds
before I was pressing my palms against
Molinari's in an exhilarated, drawn-out high
five. Deputy director or not, he had handled
himself pretty well.

"That was good, Molinari." I could hardly
contain my smile. *"And you know how
clumsy these police goons can be when
they're lugging heavy evidence. . . ."*

Our eyes locked, and suddenly I was feeling that nervousness and attraction again. I
put the car in gear. "I don't know what's supposed to happen with your contacts," I said,
"but I think we'd better start by calling this in."

Molinari speed-dialed his office with Hard-away's name and aliases. We got a quick response. His Seattle file detailed a criminal past. Weapons possession, arms theft, bank robbery. By tomorrow morning we would know everything about him.

Suddenly I realized I hadn't heard from Jill. "I gotta make a call," I said to Molinari, punching in her cell phone number.

Jill's voice mail came on. "Hi, it's District Attorney Jill Bernhardt. . . ."

Damn, Jill usually had her cell phone on. But I remembered about how she said she had a long day ahead in court. "It's me, Lindsay. It's two o' clock. Where you been?" I thought about saying more, but I wasn't in private. "Call me. I want to know how you are."

"Something wrong?" Molinari said when I hung up.

I shook my head. "A friend . . . She threw her husband out last night. We were supposed to talk. It's just that the guy's turned into a real creep."

"She's lucky, then," Molinari said, "to have a cop for a friend."

The thought amused me. Jill lucky to have a cop for a friend. I thought of calling her at the office, but she'd get back to me as soon as she turned on her phone. "Trust me, she can handle herself."

We turned on the ramp to the Bay Bridge. I didn't even have to use the top hat, as there was almost no traffic into the city. "Smooth sailing," I said. "We caught a break. Finally."

"Listen, Lindsay . . ." Molinari turned to me, his tone changed. "What do you think about having dinner with me tonight?"

"Dinner?" I thought for a second. I turned to him. "I think we know that might not be the best idea."

Molinari nodded in a resigned way, as if the thought got the better of him. "Still, we both gotta eat. . . ." He curled a smile.

Holding the wheel, I felt my palms starting to sweat. Geez. There were a hundred reasons why this could be wrong. But hell, we had lives, too.

I looked at Molinari and smiled. "We gotta eat."

Chapter 59

The latest e-mail had Cindy rocking back on her heels. For once, she was *in* the story, not just merely writing it.

And she felt a little scared. Who could blame her, with what was going on? But for the first time in her career, she also felt that she was really doing some good. And that's what thrilled her. She sucked in a deep breath and faced the screen of her computer.

That wasn't us in Portland, the message had said.

But why disclaim the killing? Why the five-word denial, nothing more?

To separate themselves. To distinguish

their crusade from a copycat killer. That seemed obvious.

But the knot growing in her stomach told her that maybe there was something more.

Maybe she was pressing too hard. But what if—completely outside the box—what if what was coming through wasn't a denial, but something else. A *conscience*.

No, that's crazy, she thought. These people had blown up Morton Lightower's town house with his wife and a child inside. They had shoved horrible poison down Bengosian's throat. But they had spared little Caitlin.

There was something else. . . . She suspected that the person corresponding might be a woman. She had referred to "her sisters in bondage." And she'd chosen to write to her. There were plenty of other reporters in the city. Why her?

Cindy was thinking that if there was any humanity in this person, maybe she could reach it. Maybe she could tap into it. Reveal something. A name, a place. Maybe it was the au pair writing, and maybe she did have a heart.

Cindy cracked her knuckles and leaned over the keyboard. Here goes . . .

She typed:

Tell me, why are you doing these things? I think you are a woman. Are you? There are better ways to achieve your goals than killing people who the world views as innocent. You can use me. I can get the message out. Please . . . I told you I was listening. I am. . . . Use me. Please . . . Don't kill anymore.

She read it over. It was a long shot. Longer than a long shot.

And she felt, pausing over the message, that if she sent it, she really would enter the story, that her whole life would change.

"Sayonara," she whispered to her old life — the one of passively watching and writing. She pressed SEND.

Chapter 60

It was hard working the rest of the day. I met with Tracchio for an hour and had Jacobi and Cappy retrace the bars around Berkeley with Hardaway's photo. Every once in a while I felt my mind drifting and my heart beating a little faster when I thought about tonight. But as Joe Molinari had said, we gotta eat.

Later, in the shower at home, inhaling a fresh lavender smell as I rinsed myself clean from the day, a guilty smile spread over my face: *Here I am, a glass of Sancerre on the ledge, my skin tingling like a girl on her first date.*

I hurried around, straightening up a bit;

arranged the bookshelf; checked the bird roasting in the oven; fed Martha; set the table overlooking the bay. Then I realized I still hadn't heard from Jill. This was crazy. Still in my towel and wet hair, I placed another call to her. "This is getting ridiculous. C'mon, get back to me. I need to know how you are. . . ."

I was about to call Claire to see if she had heard from Jill when the buzzer rang.

The front door buzzer!

Shit, it's only 7:45.

Molinari was early.

I threw another towel around my hair and frantically hopped around—dimming lights, taking out another wineglass. I finally went to the front door. "Who's there?"

"Advance team for Homeland Security," Molinari called.

"Yeah, well, you're *early,* Homeland Security. Anyone ever tell you about buzzing up from the outside door?"

"We generally bypass those things."

"Look, I'm gonna let you in, but you can't look." I couldn't believe I was standing there in my towel. "I'm opening the door."

"My eyes are closed."

"They'd better be." Martha came up beside me. "I've got a dog who's very protective of me. . . ."

I unlocked the door, opened it slowly.

Molinari stood there, his suit jacket thrown over his shoulder. A bouquet of daffodils. Eyes wide open.

"You promised." I took a step back, blushing.

"Don't blush." Molinari stood there, smiling. "You're gorgeous."

"This is Martha," I said. "You behave, Martha, or Joe'll have you tossed into a doghouse in Guantánamo. I've seen him work."

"Hey, Martha." Molinari squatted down. He massaged her head behind the ears until she closed her eyes. "You're gorgeous, too, Martha."

Molinari stood up, and I grabbed my towel tighter. He grinned a little.

"You think Martha would get upset if I said I was dying to see what's under that towel?"

I shook my head, and the towel covering my hair fell away to the floor. "How's that?"

"Not exactly what I had in mind," Molinari said.

"While you two are talking," I said, backing away, "I'll get dressed. There's wine in the fridge, vodka and scotch on the counter. And there's a bird in the oven if you have an urge to baste."

"Lindsay," Molinari said.

I stopped. "Yes . . ."

He took a step toward me. My heart stopped — except for the part that was beating violently out of control.

He put his hands on my shoulders. I felt myself shudder, then seem to sway very slightly in his hands. He put his face close. "How long did you say before that bird is ready?"

"Forty minutes." Every little hair on my arms stood on edge. "Or so."

"Too bad . . ." Molinari smiled. "But it'll have to do."

And just like that, he kissed me. His mouth was strong, and as soon as he touched my lips heat shot through me. I liked his kiss and I kissed him back. He ran his hands down the length of my back, pressed me close. I liked his touch, too. Hell, I liked *him.*

My bath towel fell to the floor.

"I have to warn you," I said. "Martha's a terror if someone gets the wrong idea."

He glanced over at Martha. She was curled up in a ball. "I don't think I have the wrong idea."

Chapter 61

Joe Molinari was facing me, and the bed-sheets were rumpled in a mess around us. I was noticing that he was even better looking up close. His eyes were deep blue and had a nice sparkle to them.

It was hard to describe how good I felt, how natural this seemed, how right. The little tremors rippling down my spine were unexpected, but definitely pleasant. It had been two years since I had felt anything like this, and that was, well . . . different. I didn't know everything about Molinari. Who was he away from the office? What did he have going on back home? Truth was, I didn't care right now. I just felt good. It was enough.

"This may seem like a strange time to ask this question," I said, "but just what is your personal situation back East?"

Molinari took a breath. "Not complicated . . . Usually I just mess around with interns and subordinates I meet on the case." He smiled.

"C'mon." I sat up. "It's a legitimate after-sex question."

"I'm divorced, Lindsay. I date now and then. Time permitting." He stroked my hair. "If you're thinking, does this happen very often . . . ?"

"What do you mean, *this?*"

"You know. *This.* Where we are. On assignment."

Molinari turned and faced me. "Just so there's no doubts, I'm here because the moment you walked into that meeting, I, well . . . bells started going off. And since then, the only thing I've been impressed with more than how good you are on the job is how good you looked once I pulled that towel off you."

I took a breath and stared into those very

blue eyes. "You just make sure you're not an asshole, Joe Molinari."

All of a sudden, I shot up in bed. "Oh my God, *dinner.*"

"Forget the chicken." Molinari smiled and pulled me closer. "We *don't* gotta eat."

The phone rang. What next?

My first urge was to let it go. I waited for the answering machine to pick up.

When the voice came on, it was Claire's, sounding urgent. "Lindsay, I'm worried. Pick up if you're there. Linds?"

I blinked, then rolled over to the night table and fumbled for my phone. "Claire. What's wrong?"

"Thank God you're home." Her voice was tense, unusual for Claire. "It's Jill. I'm at her house, Lindsay. She's not here."

"She had a trial. Did you try the office? She's probably working late."

"Of course I tried the office," Claire shot back. "Jill never showed up today."

Chapter 62

I bolted up, confused but also afraid. It didn't make sense. "She said she had a trial, Claire. I'm sure of it."

"She *did* have a trial, Lindsay. She just didn't show. They've been looking for her all day."

I pressed my back against the headboard. When I thought about the possibility of Jill bagging work, not calling in, it didn't fly.

"That's not Jill," I said.

"No," Claire answered, "that's not Jill at all."

Suddenly I was worried. "Claire, do you know what's going on? What happened with Steve?"

Claire answered, "No. What are you saying?"

"Stay where you are," I said.

I hung up the phone and sat there for a second. "I'm sorry, Joe, I gotta go."

A few minutes later I was driving at full speed down Twenty-third over to Castro. I ran through the possibilities: Jill was depressed. She needed some space. She'd gone to her parents'. Any of them could be true. But Jill would never—*never*—not show up for court.

I finally pulled up in front of her town house on Buena Vista Park. The first thing I noticed was Jill's sapphire blue 535 still in the driveway.

Claire was waiting on the landing and we hugged. "She doesn't answer," she said. "I rang the bell, banged on the door."

I looked around, didn't see anyone. "I hate to do this." Then I broke a pane in the front door and reached inside. I was thinking that Steve could have gotten inside, too—easily.

Immediately, the alarm sounded. I knew the code, 63442, Jill's state employee number. I punched it in, trying to make up my mind if the alarm being armed was a good sign.

I flicked on a light. I called, "Jill?"

Then I heard Otis barking. The brown lab ran from inside the kitchen.

"Hey, boy." I patted his back. He seemed happy to see a familiar face. "Where's Mommy?" I asked. I knew one thing. Jill would never leave him. Steve maybe, but not Otis.

"Jill . . . Steve?" I called around the house. "It's Lindsay. And Claire."

Jill had just re-done the place in the past year. Patterned couches, melon-colored walls, a tufted leather ottoman for a coffee table. The house was dark and silent. We checked around the familiar rooms. No reply. No Jill.

Claire exhaled and said, "This is really starting to give me the creeps."

I nodded and squeezed her shoulder. "Me too.

"C'mon," I said to Claire, "I'm going up to check upstairs. *We're* going to check."

Climbing the stairs, I couldn't put aside the thought of a crazed Steve charging out of some room like in some teenage horror movie. "Jill . . . Steve?" I called out again. I tugged at my gun just in case.

Still no answer. The master bedroom lights

were off. The big four-poster bed was made. Jill's toiletries and makeup in the bathroom.

When I last spoke with her she was going to bed. I was about to go back into the hallway when I saw it.

Jill's briefcase.

Jill didn't go anywhere without her "traveling office." It was a running joke. She didn't go to the beach without her goddamn work.

I took a cloth and held it by the strap, loosely. I met Claire back in the hallway. She'd checked the other rooms. "Nothing . . ."

"I don't like this, Claire. Her car's in the driveway." My eyes drifted to her case. "*This* . . . She slept here, Claire. But she never left for work."

Chapter 63

I had no idea how to get in touch with Steve.

It was late — who the hell knew where he was staying. And Jill had only been missing for the day. She could show up and be pissed over all the attention. There was nothing to do but wait and worry ourselves sick and, in my case, feel guilty.

I called Cindy and she was there in fifteen minutes. Claire called Edmund and said she was going to stay for a while, maybe the night.

We sat in Jill's den, curled up on couches. There was always the chance she'd had a change of mind and gone to visit Steve, somewhere.

Around eleven my cell phone rang. But it was only Jacobi, checking in, telling me no one in the Berkeley bars they'd checked admitted to recognizing Hardaway. Then we all sat around without speaking. I don't even remember what time we dozed off.

I woke a few times in the night, thought I heard something. "Jill?" But it wasn't her.

First thing in the morning, I went home. Joe had made the bed and left the apartment looking tidy. I showered and called in to the office to say I'd be late.

An hour later I was down at Steve's office in the Financial Center. I left the Explorer right there on the street. By the time I pushed through the office doors, I could barely control the panic I was feeling.

Steve was right there, in reception. He was practically draped over the receptionist, sipping a coffee, his leg perched casually on a chair.

"Where is she?" I said. I must've startled him because coffee splattered all over his pink Lacoste shirt.

"What the hell, Lindsay . . ." Steve held up his hands.

"Your office," I said, glaring at him hard.

"Mr. Bernhardt?" the receptionist said.

"It's okay, Stacy," Steve said. "She's a friend." *Yeah, right.*

As soon as we were down in his corner office I slammed the door. "Are you nuts, Lindsay?" Steve said.

I pushed him into a chair. "I want to know now where she is, Steve."

"Jill?" He turned up his palms and actually seemed confused.

"Cut the shit, you son of a bitch. Jill's *missing*. She didn't show up for work. I want to know where she is."

"I don't have the slightest idea," Steve said. "What do you mean, 'missing'?"

"She had a trial yesterday, Steve," I said, losing control, "and she didn't show up for it. Does that sound like Jill? She didn't come home last night, either. Her car's there. And her briefcase. *Someone got inside the house.*"

"I think you've got your facts a little twisted, Lieutenant," Steve said with a derisive laugh. "Jill tossed me out the other night. She changed the locks on Fortress Bernhardt."

"Don't mess with me, Steve. I want to

know what you've done. When was the last time you saw her?"

"How about eleven o'clock the other night, through my own living-room window, as I was banging on the fucking door, trying to get back into my own house?"

"She told me you were coming by yesterday morning to pick up your things."

Anger flashed in his eyes. "What the hell is this, an interrogation?"

"I want to know where you spent Friday night"—I stared at him hard—"and everything you did Saturday morning before you came to work."

"What's going on? Do I need a lawyer, Lindsay?"

I didn't answer his question, just turned away and walked out of there. I hoped to God Steve *didn't* need a lawyer.

Chapter 64

Anger was no longer the word for what was tearing at me as I headed back to the Hall. It was deeper than anger. Every time I glanced in the rearview mirror and caught a glimpse of my own eyes, I kept thinking, *I've seen those eyes before.*

On the job. On the faces of parents and wives when someone close to them is missing. The wordless panic when something horrible has taken place but just hasn't played out yet. *Stay calm,* we tell them. *Anything can happen. It's still early.*

And that's what I was telling myself as I

drove back to the office. Stay calm, Lindsay. Jill could turn up anytime. . . .

But looking at myself in the rearview mirror, I couldn't stop thinking, *Same eyes.*

Back at the Hall, I put in a call to Ingrid Barros, who was Jill's housekeeper, but she was at a meeting at her kid's school. I sent Lorraine and Chin up and down Jill's street on Buena Vista Park to see if anyone had noticed anything suspicious. I even ordered a trace on Jill's cell phone calls.

Someone must have called her. *Someone* must have seen her. It didn't make sense that she had completely disappeared. Jill wasn't the disappearing type.

I did my best to focus on the picture we were getting on Stephen Hardaway as it started to drift in throughout the day. The FBI had been looking for Hardaway for a couple of years, and though he wasn't on the Most Wanted, he was close enough to raise suspicions now.

He'd been raised in Lansing, Michigan. After high school, he came west and went to Reed College in Portland. That's when he began turning up in the system. Oregon records showed an arrest for aggravated assault at an anti-WTO demonstration at the University of Oregon. He was a suspect in bank robberies in Eugene and Seattle. Then in '99, he was caught in Arizona trying to buy blasting caps from a gang member who turned out to be local ATF. And that was when Stephen Hardaway disappeared. He'd jumped bail. He was rumored to be involved in a string of armed robberies in Washington and Oregon. So we knew he was armed, dangerous, and had a desire to blow things up.

Not a word on him for the past two years.

About five, Claire knocked at my office. "I'm going crazy, Lindsay. C'mon, get a cup of coffee with me."

"I'm going crazy, too," I said, and grabbed my purse. "Maybe we should call Cindy over," I said.

"Don't bother," she said, and pointed down the hall. "She's already here."

The three of us went down to a cafeteria on the second floor. At first we just sat around stirring our drinks, the silence as thick as June fog.

Finally I just sucked in a breath. "I think we all agree, Jill's not out there, pining away on some rock. Something's happened. The sooner we admit that, the sooner we can find out what it is."

"I keep thinking there has to be some explanation," Claire said. "I mean, I know Steve. We all do. He wouldn't be my ideal partner, but I can't believe he's capable of anything like this."

"Well, keep believing," Cindy said, frowning, "it's been two days."

Claire looked at me. "You remember that time Jill had to go through Salt Lake City on her way back from Atlanta, and while they were just waiting there at the gate, she took one look at all the snow in the mountains and said, 'Screw it, I'm outta here!' She hopped off the plane, rented a car, and skied Snowbird for the day."

"Yeah, I remember," I said, the thought bringing a smile to my face. "Steve had some client thing he wanted to drag her to, the office was trying to locate her, and where was Jill? Up at eleven thousand feet, in a rented suit and skis, in powder heaven. Having the best day of her life."

The image brought a smile to all our faces, a tearful one.

"So that's what I think." Claire took a napkin and dabbed her eyes. "I think she's skiing powder. I have to believe she's skiing powder, Lindsay."

Chapter 65

Cindy stayed at her desk late that night, when only a handful of Metro stringers trolling the police wires were still around. The truth was, where else could she go?

This thing with Jill was killing her; it was killing all of them.

Word had leaked out. A missing A.D.A. was news. Her city editor asked if she wanted to write it. He knew they were friends. "It's not news yet," she had snapped. Writing it made it news. Made it real.

This time it wasn't happening to someone else.

She stared at a photo of them she kept

taped to her cubicle. The four of them, in
their old haunt, Susie's, their corner booth,
after they solved the bride and groom case.
A few margaritas had left their brains leaking
like a wetlands preserve. Jill had seemed so
invincible. The power job, the power husband. Never once had she let on. . . .

"C'mon, Jill," Cindy whispered, feeling her
eyes glistening over. *Come through this.
Walk through that door. Show your pretty
face, smiling. I'm praying, Jill. Walk through
that fucking door.*

It was after eleven. Nothing was happening here. It was just her way of keeping the
vigil, keeping up hope. *Go home, Cindy. Call
it a night. Nothing you can do now.*

A maintenance man vacuuming the stall
winked at her. "Working late, Ms. Thomas?"

"Yeah," she sighed, "burning the midnight
oil."

She finally threw a few things in her purse
and checked her computer one last time
before she logged off. Maybe she'd call Lindsay. Just to talk.

A new e-mail flashed on her screen.

Cindy knew without even opening it who it
was from. Toobad@hotmail.com.

She knew the timing. She knew they

warned her of a new victim every three days. It was Sunday. August Spies were due.

"You were warned," the message began. "But you were arrogant and didn't listen."

Oh God. A tiny cry escaped from Cindy's throat.

She flashed down the screen, reading the terrifying message, the chilling signature at the end.

August Spies had struck again.

Chapter 66

I got home that night at eleven, exhausted and empty-handed. For a few moments I stood thinking at the bottom of the outside stairs. In the morning, Jill would be officially listed as "missing." I'd have to head up an investigation into the disappearance of one of my closest friends.

"I thought you'd want to know"—I heard a voice above me, catching me by surprise—"I heard back from Portland."

I looked up and saw Molinari; he was sitting on the top step.

"They found a secretary at Portland State who leaked Propp's whereabouts to a boyfriend. They traced the gun to him. Local radical. But I suspect that's not going to cheer you up much tonight."

"I thought you were supposed to be somebody important, Molinari," I said, too empty and tired to show how glad I was to see him. "How come you always end up babysitting me?"

He stood up. "I didn't want you to feel you have to be alone."

Suddenly I just couldn't hold back. The floodgates burst, and he came down and held me. Molinari drew me to him tightly as the tears carved their way down my cheeks. I felt ashamed to let him see me like this—I wanted so badly to appear strong—but I couldn't get the tears to stop.

"I'm sorry," I said, trying to catch myself.

"No"—he stroked my hair—"you don't have to pretend with me. You can let it out. There's no shame."

Something's happened to Jill! I wanted to scream, but I was afraid to lift my face.

"I'm sorry, too." He held me close. Then he squeezed me gently by the shoulders and looked into my swollen eyes. "I was with the Department of Justice," he said, and brushed away a few tears, "when the Trade

Towers fell. I knew guys who were killed. Some of the fire chiefs, John O'Neill in Trade Center Security. I was one of the heads of the emergency response team, but when all the names started coming in, people I'd worked with, I couldn't take it anymore. I went into the men's room. I knew everything was on the line. But I sat in a stall and cried. There's no shame."

I unlocked the front door and we went inside. Molinari made me tea as I sat curled up on the couch, Martha's chin on my thigh. I didn't know what I would do if I was alone. He came over and poured it for me. I nestled into him, the tea warming me, his arms draped around my shoulders. And we just sat there for a long time. He was right, too — there's no shame.

"Thank you," I sighed into his chest.

"For what? Knowing how to make tea?"

"Just thank you. For not being one of the assholes." I closed my eyes. For a moment, everything bad was outside, far away from my living room.

The telephone rang. I didn't want to answer it. For a moment, I was feeling a million miles away and, selfish as it was, I liked it.

Then I was thinking, *What if it's Jill?*

I grabbed the phone and Cindy's voice came on. "Lindsay, thank God. Something bad's happened."

My body clenched. I held on to Molinari. "Jill?"

"No," she answered, "August Spies."

Chapter 67

I listened with a sick, sinking feeling as Cindy read me the latest message. " 'You were warned,' it says. 'But you were arrogant and didn't listen. We're not surprised. You've never listened before. So we struck again.' Lindsay, it's signed August Spies."

"There's been another killing," I said, turning to Molinari. Then I finished up with Cindy.

The full message said we'd find what we were looking for at 333 Harrison Street, down by the piers in Oakland. It had been *exactly* three days since Cindy received the first e-mail. August Spies were true to their threats.

I hung up with Cindy and called the Emergency Task Force. I wanted our cops on the scene, and all traffic down to the Oakland port blocked off. I had no idea what type of incident we had or how many lives were involved, so I called Claire and told her to go there, too.

Molinari already had his jacket on and was on the phone. It took me about a minute to get ready. "C'mon," I said at the door, "you might as well drive with me."

We were barreling down Third Street toward the bridge with our siren wailing. That time of night there was almost no traffic. It was clear sailing over the Bay Bridge.

Transmissions began to crackle on the radio. Oakland cops had picked up the 911. Molinari and I listened to hear what kind of scene we were dealing with: fire, explosion, multiple injuries?

I shot off the bridge onto 880, getting off at the exit for the port. A police checkpoint had already been set up. Two patrol cars with flashing lights. We pulled up. I saw Cindy's purple VW being held there. She was arguing with one of the officers.

"Climb in!" I yelled to her. Molinari flashed

his badge to a young patrolman, whose eyes bulged. "She's with us."

From the exit ramp it was only a short drive down to the port. Harrison Street was right off the piers. Cindy explained how she had received the e-mail. She'd brought a copy, and Molinari read as we drove.

As we neared the port, flashing green and red lights were all over the place. It seemed as if every cop in Oakland was on the scene. "C'mon, we're getting out here."

The three of us jumped out and ran toward an old brick warehouse marked 333. Trestles rose into the night. Huge container loads were stacked everywhere. The port of Oakland actually handled the majority of the freight traffic in the Bay Area.

I heard my name being called. Claire, jumping out of her Pathfinder, ran up to us. "What do we have?"

"I don't know yet," I said.

Finally I saw an Oakland precinct captain I'd worked with coming out of the building. "Gene!" I ran up to him. With what was going on, I didn't have to ask.

"The victim's dumped on the second floor. Single shot to the back of the head."

Part of me winced, part of me relaxed. At least it was only one.

We headed up steep metal stairs, Claire and Cindy following behind. An Oakland cop tried to stop us. I pushed my badge at him and moved past. A body was on the floor, partially wrapped in a bloody tarp. "Goddammit," I said. "Those bastards." Two cops and an EMS team were leaning over the victim.

There was a note fastened by a metal twist to the tarp. A bill of lading.

"'You were warned,'" I read it out loud. "'The criminal state is not exempt from its own crimes. Members of the G-8, come to your senses. Renounce the colonizing policies. You have three more days. We can strike anywhere, anytime. August Spies.'"

At the bottom of the page I saw the words in bold print, RETURN THIS TO THE HALL OF JUSTICE.

My body stopped dead. A wave of panic tore at me. For a second I couldn't move. I looked at Claire. Her face crumpled with shock.

I pushed an EMT out of the way. I went down on my knees. The first thing I came

upon was the victim's wrist—the aquama-
rine David Yurman bracelet I knew so well.
"Oh no," I gasped. "No, no, no . . ."
I peeled back the tarp.
It was Jill.

Part Four

Chapter 68

Thinking back, I remember only flashes of what happened next. I know I stood there, unable to comprehend what I was seeing: Jill's beautiful face, lifeless now. Her eyes staring forward, clear, almost serene. "Oh no, no . . . ," I repeated over and over.

I know my legs gave out, and someone held me. Claire's voice, cracking: "Oh my God, Lindsay . . ."

I couldn't take my eyes off Jill's face. A trickle of blood seeped from the corner of her mouth. I reached out and touched her hand. She still had her wedding ring on.

I heard Cindy start to cry, and saw Claire

holding her. I kept repeating over and over, *This can't be Jill. What does she have to do with August Spies?*

Then things fell into a daze. I kept reminding myself, *It's a crime scene, Lindsay, a homicide scene.* I wanted to be strong for Claire and Cindy, for all the cops around. I asked, "Did anyone see how she got here?" I looked around. "I want the area canvassed. Someone could've seen a vehicle."

Molinari tried to pull me away, but I shook him off. I had to look around, find something. There was always something, some mistake they had made. *You assholes, August Spies . . . You scum.*

Suddenly Jacobi was there. And Cappy. Even Tracchio. My homicide team. "Let us handle it," Cappy said. Finally, I just let them take charge.

I was beginning to understand that this was real. These emergency lights, they weren't in my head. Jill was dead. She'd been killed, not by Steve but by August Spies.

I watched them take her away. My friend. Jill . . . I watched Claire help place her into the morgue van and send it off, sirens blaring. Joe Molinari comforted me as best he could, but then he had to return to the Hall.

Then as the crime scene quieted down, Claire, Cindy, and I sat on the steps of an adjoining building in the light rain. Not a word passed between us. My brain echoed with questions I couldn't answer: *Why? How does this fit? It's a different case! How can Jill be connected?*

How long we sat on those steps I don't know. The haze of urgent voices, flashing lights. Cindy weeping, Claire holding her. Me too stunned to even speak, my fists clenched, turning the question over and over. *Why?*

A thought kept creeping into my head. *If only I had gone to Jill's that night. None of this might have been. . . .*

Suddenly a ringing broke the silence. Cindy's cell. She answered, her voice tremulous. "Yes?" Cindy drew a breath. "I'm at the scene."

It was her Metro desk.

In a halting voice, she gave details of what had taken place. "Yes, it looks like it *is* part of the terror campaign. The third victim . . ." She described the location, the e-mail she had received at the paper, the time.

Then Cindy stopped. I could see tears glazing her eyes. She bit her lip, as if she was afraid to let the words out. "Yes, the victim's been identified. Her name is Bernhardt . . . Jill." She spelled it letter by letter.

She tried to say something else, but the words caught in her throat. Claire reached for her. Cindy sucked in a breath, wiped her eyes. "Yes," she said, nodding. "Ms. Bernhardt was Chief Assistant District Attorney of the City of San Francisco. . . ."

Then, in a whisper, "She was also my friend."

Chapter 69

I knew I wouldn't be able to sleep that night.
I didn't want to go home.

So I stayed at the crime scene until the lab
teams had come and gone; then for about
an hour I crisscrossed the deserted streets
of the port searching for anyone, a night
worker, a vagrant, who might've seen who
dumped Jill off. I drove around, afraid to go
to the office, afraid to go home, reliving the
awful sight over and over again, tears
streaming down my face. Turning over that
tarp — seeing Jill!

I drove until my car seemed to know the
place I was headed. Where else did I have to

go? Three o'clock in the morning. I found myself at the morgue.

I knew Claire would be there. No matter what time it was. Doing her job because it was the one thing that could hold her together. In her blue scrubs, in the operating room.

Jill was laid out on the gurney. Under those same harsh lights where I'd seen so many victims before.

Jill . . . My sweet darling girl.

I stared through the glass, tears wending down my cheeks. I was thinking I'd failed her in some way.

Finally I pushed through the glass doors. Claire was in the middle of the autopsy. She was doing what I was doing. Her job.

"You don't want to be in here, Lindsay," she said when she saw me. She drew a sheet over Jill's exposed wound.

"Yeah, I do, Claire." I just stood there. I wasn't going to leave. I needed to see this.

Claire stared at my swollen, tear-stained face. She nodded, the tiny outline of a smile. "At least make yourself useful and hand me that probe on the tray over there."

I handed Claire her instrument and traced

the back of my hand against Jill's cold, hard cheek. *How could this not be some dream?*

"Widespread damage to the right occipital lobe," Claire spoke into the microphone on her lapel, "consistent with a single, rear-entry gunshot trauma. No exit wound; the bullet is still lodged in the left lateral ventricle. Minimal blood loss to the affected area. Strange . . . ," she muttered.

I was barely listening. My eyes still fixed on Jill.

"Light powder burns around the hair and neck indicate a small-caliber weapon fired at close range," Claire continued.

She shifted the body. The opened rear of Jill's skull appeared on the monitor.

I *couldn't* watch that. I looked away.

"I'm now removing what looks like a small-caliber bullet fragment from the left ventricle," Claire went on. "Signs of severe rupture, symptomatic of this type of trauma, but . . . very little swelling . . ." I watched Claire as she probed around and removed a flattened bullet. She dropped it into a dish.

A jolt of rage tensed me. It looked like a flattened .22. Caked with specks of Jill's blood.

"Something doesn't fit," Claire said, puzzled. She looked up at me. "This area ought to be covered in spinal fluid. No swelling of the brain tissue, very little blood."

Suddenly Claire the professional clicked in. "I'm going to open up the chest cavity," she spoke into the mike. "Lindsay, look away."

"What's wrong, Claire? What's going on?"

"Something's not right." Claire rolled the body over, took out a scalpel. Then she slipped the blade down a straight line from the top of Jill's chest.

I did avert my eyes. I didn't want to see Jill like that.

"I'm doing a standard sternotomy," Claire dictated into the mike. "Opening up the pneumo chest area. Lung membrane is soft, tissue . . . degraded, soupy . . . I'm exposing the pericardium now. . . ." I heard Claire take a deep breath. *"Shit."*

My heart started racing. I was fixed on the screen now. "Claire, what's going on? What do you see?"

"Stay there." She put up a hand. She had seen something horrible. What was it?

"Oh, Lindsay," she whispered, and finally looked at me. "Jill didn't die from a gunshot."

"What!"

"The lack of swelling, blood seepage." She shook her head. "The gunshot was delivered after she was dead."

"What are you saying, Claire?"

"I'm not sure"—she looked up—"but if I had to guess . . . I'd say ricin."

Chapter 70

There was always something intimidating about meeting Charles Danko in person. Even at a fancy place like the Huntington Hotel in San Francisco. Danko fit in anywhere. He was wearing a tweed jacket, pinstriped shirt, and a rep tie.

There was a girl with him, pretty, with a tangle of bright red hair. He always liked to keep you off guard. *Who is she?*

Mal had been told to wear a suit jacket and even a tie, if he could dig one up. He had, and he found it kind of funny—bright red with tiny bugles in the design.

Danko stood rather formally and shook

Mal's hand, just another of his odd off-putting gestures. He waved a hand around the dining room. "Could there be a safer place for us to meet? My Gawd, *the Huntington!*"

He looked at the girl and they both laughed, but he didn't introduce her.

"Ricin," Malcolm said, "it's *brilliant.* What a great day—we got Bengosian! We can do so much damage here. Hell, we could wipe out *this* capitalist den in about a minute flat. Go over to the Mark and take out another hundred rich bloodsuckers. Take the trolley and spring death on anybody we passed."

"Yes, especially because I figured how to make it as a concentrate."

Malcolm nodded, but he looked nervous. "I thought this was about G-8?"

Danko looked at the girl again. They shared condescending smiles. *Who the hell is she? What does she know?*

"Your focus is too narrow, Mal. We've talked about that before. More than anything else, this is about terrifying people. And we're going to scare them, believe me. Ricin will do the trick. Makes anthrax look like something only farm animals should fret about."

He stared hard at Malcolm now. "You have a delivery system for me? For the ricin?"

Malcolm had stopped making eye contact. "Yeah."

"And more of your explosives?"

"We could blow the Huntington right off the map. The Mark, too." Malcolm finally allowed himself a sheepish smile. "All right, who is *she?*"

Danko threw back his head and laughed. "She's someone brilliant, just like you. She's a secret weapon. Let's leave it at that. Just another soldier," he said, then looked into the girl's eyes. "There's always another soldier, Malcolm. That's what should be scaring the hell out of everybody right now."

Chapter 71

Michelle heard voices in the other room. Mal was back from his meeting. Julia was whooping it up as if she'd won the lottery. But Michelle felt awful.

She knew they had done terrible things. The latest killing didn't sit well with her. That pretty, innocent D.A. She had put aside the image of Charlotte Lightower and the housekeeper who'd been killed in the blast, and found some relief that at least the children had been saved. Lightower, Bengosian — they were greedy, guilty scum.

But this one. What had she done to be on the list? Because she worked for the state?

What had Mal said? *This one is just for the thrill of it, just to show we can.* Except Michelle didn't really believe that. There was always a hidden agenda with Mal.

The poor D.A. knew she was going to die from the minute they forced her into the truck. But she never gave in. Not once. She seemed brave to Michelle. The real crime was that she never even knew why she was dying! They wouldn't even give her that.

The door creaked open and Mal eased into the room. The look of triumph on his face gave Michelle the creeps. He lay down next to her, smelling of tobacco and alcohol. "What happened to my party girl?"

"Not tonight," Michelle said. A wheeze kicked up in her chest.

"Not tonight?" Mal grinned.

Michelle sat up. "I just don't understand. Why her? What did she do to anybody?"

"I mean, what did any of them really do?" Mal stroked her hair. "Wrong employer, honeybun. She represented the big bad state that's sanctioning the criminal pillaging of the world. That's what she did, Michelle. She's tanks in Iraq. She's Grumman and Dow Chemical and the WTO all rolled into one. Don't be fooled because she was pretty."

"They said on the news that she put away murderers. She even prosecuted some of these CEOs in business scandals."

"And I told you *not* to pay attention to the news, Michelle. Sometimes people who do good things die. Hold that thought."

She shot a horrified look at him. The cough in her chest grew tighter. She fumbled around the bed for her new inhaler, but Mal blocked her hand. "What did you think, Michelle? We were in this just to knock off a couple of fat-cat billionaires? Our fight's with the state. The state is very powerful. It won't roll over and die."

Michelle forced a breath. She realized in that moment that she was different from Mal. From them all. He called her a little girl. But he was wrong. A little girl didn't do the terrible things she had done. She wheezed again. "I need my inhaler, Mal. Please."

"And I need to know if I can trust you, honeybun." He picked up the inhaler and twirled it in his fingers like a toy.

Her breathing was starting to get heavy now, ragged. And Mal was making it worse, scaring her like this. She didn't know what he was capable of. "You can trust me, Mal. You know that," she whispered.

"I do know that, Michelle, but it's not *me* I'm worried about. I mean, we work for someone, don't we, hon? Charles Danko isn't forgiving, the way I am. Danko is tough enough to beat them at their own game. He's a genius."

She grabbed the puffer out of Mal's hand and depressed it twice, shooting the soothing spray into her lungs.

"You know the cool thing about ricin?" Mal smiled. "It can get into your bloodstream a hundred ways." He depressed his index finger twice, as though he was triggering an imaginary inhaler. He smiled. *"Chht, chht."*

He had a glint in his eye she hadn't seen before. "Whoa, now that would *really* get that chest of yours into a state, wouldn't it, hon? *Chht, chht."*

Chapter 72

It was bedlam at the Hall that morning. As scary as it had ever been since I entered police work.

An A.D.A. being killed. August Spies' victim number three.

By six A.M., the place was teeming with a hundred Feds: FBI, Department of Justice, ATF. And reporters, crammed into the fifth-floor news room for some kind of briefing. The front page of the *Examiner* had a big banner headline: WHO'S NEXT?

I was going over one of the crime scene reports from Jill's killing when I was surprised by Joe Santos and Phil Martelli knocking at my door. "We're real sorry to hear about Ms. Bernhardt," Santos said, stepping in.

I tossed aside the papers and nodded thanks. "It was nice of you to come here."

Martelli shrugged. "Actually, that's not why we're here, Lindsay."

"We decided to go back through our records on this Hardaway thing," Santos said, sitting down. He pulled out a manila envelope. "We figured if he was here, given what he was up to, he had to turn up somewhere else."

Santos removed a series of black-and-white photos from the envelope. "This is a rally we were keeping track of. October twenty-second. Six months ago."

The photos were surveillance sweeps of the crowd, no one in particular. Then one face was circled. Sandy hair, a narrow chin, a thin beard. Huddled in a dark fatigue jacket, jeans, a scarf that hung to his knees.

My blood started to race. I went up to my board and compared it with the FBI photos taken in Seattle five years before.

Stephen Hardaway.

The son of a bitch was *here* six months ago.

"This is where it starts to get interesting."
Phil Martelli winked.

He spread out a couple of other shots. A different rally. Hardaway again. This time, standing next to someone I recognized.

Roger Lemouz.

Hardaway had an arm around him.

Chapter 73

Half an hour later I pulled up on Durant Avenue at the south entrance to the university. I ran inside Dwinelle Hall, where Lemouz had his office.

The professor was there, outfitted in a tweed jacket and white linen shirt, entertaining a coed with flowing red hair.

"Party's over," I said.

"Ah, Madam Lieutenant." He smiled. That condescending accent, Etonian or Oxfordian or whatever the hell it was. "I was just counseling Annette here on how Foucault says that the same forces which historically depress class affect gender, too."

"Well, class is over, Red." I flashed the student an "I don't want to see you in here in about ten seconds" look. It took her about that long to gather her books and leave. To her credit, Red flashed me a middle finger at the door. I returned the favor.

"I'm delighted to see you again." Lemouz seemed not to mind and pushed back in his chair. "Given the sad affairs on the news this morning, I fear the subject is politics — not women's development."

"I think I misjudged you, Lemouz." I remained standing. "I thought you were just some pompous two-bit agitator, and you turn out to be a real player."

Lemouz crossed his legs and gave me a condescending smile. "I'm not sure I understand what you mean."

I took out the envelope with Santos's photos.

"What I'm really getting a kick out of, Lemouz, is that *I'm* what's keeping your ass away from Homeland Security. I pass along your name, with your public statements, the next time I see you, it'll be in a cell."

Lemouz leaned back in his chair, still with an amused smile. "And you're warning me, *why,* Lieutenant?"

"Who said I am warning you?"

His expression changed. He had no idea what I had on him. I liked that.

"What I find amusing"—Lemouz shook his head—"is how your blessed Constitution is so blind to people in this country who are wearing a chador or who have the wrong accent, yet so high and mighty about the threat to a free society when it comes to a couple of greedy MBAs and a pretty D.A."

I pretended I hadn't even heard what he just said.

"There's something I want you to look at, Lemouz."

I opened the envelope and spread the FBI photos of Stephen Hardaway across the desk.

Lemouz shrugged. "I don't know. Perhaps I've seen him. . . . I don't know where. Is he a student here?"

"You weren't listening, Lemouz." I dropped another photo in front of him. A second. And a third. The ones taken by Santos and Martelli. Showing Hardaway standing with him, one with his arm draped across the professor's shoulder. "How do I find him, Lemouz? *How?*"

He shook his head. "I don't know. These photos are from some time ago. I believe he was a professor detained after nine-eleven. Last fall. He hung around a couple of our rallies. I haven't seen him since. I don't actually know the man."

"That's not good enough," I pressed.

"I don't know. That's the truth, Lieutenant. He was from up north somewhere, as I remember. Eugene? Seattle? He hung around for a while, but it all seemed to bore him."

For once, I believed Lemouz. "What name was he going under?"

"Not Hardaway. Malcolm something. Malcolm Dennis, I think. I don't know where he is now. No idea."

There was part of me that liked seeing Lemouz's slick, superior veneer crack. "I want to know one more thing. And this stays between us. Okay?"

Lemouz nodded. "Of course."

"The name August Spies. You know it?"

Lemouz blinked. The color came back to his face. "That's what they're calling themselves?"

I sat down and pushed myself close to

him. We had never let the name out before. *And he knew.* I could see it on his face.

"Tell me, Lemouz. Who are the August Spies?"

Chapter 74

"Have you ever heard of the Haymarket Massacre?" he asked me, talking as if I were one of his students.

"You mean in Chicago?" I said.

"Very good, Lieutenant." Lemouz nodded. "To this day, there is a statue there. To mark it. On May first, 1886, there was a massive labor demonstration up Michigan Avenue. The greatest gathering of labor to that point in the history of the United States. Eighty thousand workers, women and children too. To this day, May Day is celebrated as labor's official holiday around the globe. Everywhere, of course," he said with a smirk, *"but in the United States."*

"Cut to the chase. I don't need the politics."

"The demonstration was peaceful," Lemouz went on, "and over the next couple of days, more and more workers went out on strike and rallied. Then, on the third day, the police fired into the crowd. Two protestors were killed. The next day another demonstration was organized. At Haymarket Square. Randolph and Des Plaines Streets.

"Angry speeches blasted the government. The mayor ordered the police to disperse the crowd. One hundred seventy-six Chicago cops entered the square in a phalanx and stormed the crowd, wielding their nightsticks. Then the police opened fire. When the dust settled, seven police and four demonstrators lay dead.

"The police needed scapegoats, so they rounded up eight labor leaders, some of whom were not even there that day."

"Where is this heading?"

"One of them was a teacher named August Spies. They tried and hanged them all. By the neck. Until dead. Later on, Spies was shown not to have even been at Haymarket. He said, as he stood on the scaffold,

'If you think that by hanging us you can stamp out the labor movement, then hang us. The ground is on fire where you stand. *Let the voice of the people be heard.'*"

Lemouz stared deeply into my eyes. "A moment barely recorded in the history of your country, Lieutenant, but one that would inspire. One that apparently has."

Chapter 75

People were going to die here soon. Quite a lot of people, actually.

Charles Danko sat pretending to read the *Examiner* underneath the giant fountain in the sparkling glass atrium of the Rincon Center just off Market Street, downtown near the Bay Bridge. From above him, an eighty-five-foot plume of water splashed breathtakingly into a shallow pool.

Americans like to feel awe, he thought to himself—they liked it in their movies, their pop art, and even their shopping centers. *So I'll make them feel awe. I'll make them feel in awe of death.*

It would be busy here today, Danko knew. The Rincon Center's restaurants were getting ready for the surge of the lunch crowd. A thousand or more escapees from law firms and real estate trusts and financial advisers around the Financial District.

Too bad this can't stretch out a little longer, Charles Danko thought, and sighed, the regret of someone who has waited such a long time for the moment. The Rincon Center had proved to be one of his favorite places in San Francisco.

Danko didn't acknowledge the well-dressed black man who picked out a place beside him facing the fountain. He knew the man was a veteran of the Gulf War. Despondent ever since. Dependable, though perhaps a little high-strung.

"Mal said I could call you 'Professor.'" The black spoke out of the side of his mouth.

"And you are Robert?" Danko asked.

The man nodded. "Robert I am."

A woman started to play on a grand piano in the center of the atrium. Every day at ten to twelve. A melody from *Phantom of the Opera* began to fill the gigantic space.

"You know who to look for?" Danko asked.

"I know," the man said, assured. "I'll do my

job. You don't have to worry about me. I'm a very good soldier."

"It must be the right man," Danko said. "You'll see him come into the square at about twenty after twelve. He'll cross it, maybe drop some change off for the pianist. Then he'll go into Yank Sing."

"You seem awfully sure he'll be here."

Danko finally looked at the man and smiled. "You see that plume of water, Robert? It falls from a height of precisely eighty-five point five feet. I know this because having sat in this spot for a very long time, I have calculated the exact angle of an imaginary line stretching from the center of the pool, and the corresponding right angle created at its base. From there, it was easy to extrapolate its height. You know how many days I've sat and watched this fountain, Robert? Don't you worry, he'll be there."

Charles Danko stood up. He left behind the briefcase. "I thank you, Robert. You are doing something very brave. Something that only a small few will ever commend you for. Good luck, my friend. You're a hero today."

And you're serving my purpose as well.

Chapter 76

On a dank, drizzly afternoon in Highland Park, Texas, we said good-bye to Jill. I had said good-bye to people I loved before. But I had never felt so empty or numb. And never so cheated.

The temple was a modern brick-and-glass structure with a steep-angled sanctuary filled with light. The rabbi was a woman, and Jill would've liked that. Everyone flew down. Chief Tracchio, D.A. Sinclair. Some associates from the office. Claire, Cindy, and me. A group of girls from high school and college Jill had kept in touch with over the years.

Steve was there, of course, though I couldn't bear to speak to him.

We took our seats, and an aria from *Turandot,* Jill's favorite, was sung by a local choir.

Bennett Sinclair said a few words. He praised Jill as the most dedicated prosecutor on his staff. "People said she was tough. And she was tough. But not so tough that respect and humanity were ever casualties in how she conducted herself. Most of us have lost a good friend"—he pressed his lips—"but the city of San Francisco is going to miss one hell of a lawyer."

A classmate from Stanford showed a picture of Jill on the women's soccer team that went to the national finals, and made the crowd laugh when she said it didn't take long to know who really had it together, as Jill was the only one on the team who joked that "doubling up" meant carrying two majors.

I got up and spoke briefly. "Everyone knew Jill Meyer Bernhardt as this self-assured, achieving winner. Top of her law school class. Strongest conviction rate on the D.A.'s staff. Free-climbed the Sultan's Spire in Moab," I said. "I knew her for all those things, too, but mostly as a friend whose deepest inner wish wasn't about convictions or big cases but simply to bring a child into this world. That was the Jill I loved best, the real Jill."

Claire played the cello. She slowly climbed the platform and sat there for a while, then the choir joined in the background in a hauntingly beautiful version of "Loving Arms," one of Jill's favorite songs. How many times we used to sing that song, meeting after work at Susie's, straining in margarita-drenched harmony. I watched Claire close her eyes, and the tremors of the cello and the softly singing voices in the background were the perfect tribute to Jill.

As the final verse began, the pallbearers picked up the casket, and Jill's family reluctantly rose to follow.

And as they did, a few of us began to clap our hands. Slowly at first, as the procession walked by. Then one by one, everyone joined in.

As the casket neared the rear doors, the pallbearers stopped and held it for a few seconds, as if to make sure Jill could hear her tribute.

I was looking at Claire. Tears were streaming down my face so hard, I thought they would never stop. I wanted to shout out, *Go, Jill.* . . . Claire squeezed my hand. Then Cindy squeezed the other.

And I thought to myself, *I'll find the bastard, Jill. You sleep easy.*

Chapter 77

It was after midnight by the time Cindy got home. Her eyes were raw, her body numb, and she wondered if she would ever recover from losing Jill.

She knew she wouldn't be able to sleep. The answering machine was blinking. She'd been out of touch all day. She ought to check her e-mail, maybe just to get Jill off her mind.

She went to her computer and checked out the *Chronicle*'s front page. The story of the day was ricin. Jill's COD had gotten out. Her death, coupled with Bengosian's, had put the city in a panic. How easily could ricin be obtained? What were the symptoms? What if it got into the water supply? Were there antidotes? How many people could die in San Francisco?

She was about to check her e-mail when an Instant Message bubbled through. Hotwax1199.

Don't waste your time trying to trace this, the message began.

Cindy froze.

No need to even write it down. It belongs to a sixth-grader in Dublin, Ohio. He doesn't even know it's gone. His name is Marion Delgado, the message continued. Do you know who I am?

Yes, Cindy wrote back. I know who you are. You're the son of a bitch who killed my friend Jill. Why are you contacting me?

There's going to be another strike, the answer appeared.

Tomorrow. Not like before. A lot of innocent people are going to die. Completely innocent people.

Where? Cindy typed. She waited anxiously. Can you tell me where? Please!

This G-8 meeting has to be canceled, the message returned.

You said you wanted to help, so help, goddamnit! These people, the government, they have to own up to their crimes. Murdering innocent people, just for oil. Multinationals on the loose, preying on the poor across the world. You said you wanted to get our message across. Here's your chance. Make these thieves and murderers stop their crimes now.

There was a silence. Cindy wasn't sure if the messenger was still there. She didn't know what to do next.

More words appeared on her screen.

Get them to acknowledge their crimes. It's the only way to stop these deaths.

This was something else, Cindy was thinking. The writer was reaching out. Maybe a sliver of guilt, or reason, holding back the insanity.

I can tell you want to stop this insanity, Cindy wrote.

Please, tell me what's going to happen. No one has to get hurt!

Nothing. No further reply came.

"Shit!" Cindy pounded the keyboard. They were using her, that's all. To get their message out.

She typed:

Why did Jill Bernhardt have to die? What

crime did she commit? Stealing oil? Globalization? What did she do?

A full thirty seconds elapsed. Then a
minute. Cindy was sure she had lost the
messenger. She shouldn't have gotten mad.
This was bigger than her anger or her grief.

She finally rested her head against the
monitor. When she looked up, she couldn't
believe it. More words had appeared.

Jill Bernhardt didn't have anything to do with
G-8. This one wasn't like the others. This one
was personal, the message read.

Chapter 78

Something terrible was going to happen today. Cindy's latest e-mail assured us of that. And her strange pen pal hadn't been wrong yet, hadn't misled her or lied.

It was a sickening, helpless feeling to watch the dawn creep into the sky and know: in spite of all the resources of the U.S. government, all the fancy vigilance and warnings and cops we could put out on the street, all my years of solving homicides . . . August Spies were going to strike today. We couldn't do a thing to stop the killers.

That dawn found me in the city's Emergency Command Center, one of those "undisclosed locations" hidden in a nondescript cinder-block building in a remote section of the naval yard out in Hunter's Point. It was a large room filled with monitors and high-tech communications equipment. Everyone there was on edge. What were August Spies going to pull now?

Joe Molinari was there. The mayor, Tracchio, the heads of the fire department and Emergency Medical Task Force, all of us crammed around the "war table."

Claire was there, too. The latest warning had everyone freaked out that this new attack could be a widespread one involving ricin. Molinari had a toxins expert on alert.

During the night we had decided to release Hardaway's name and description to the press. So far we hadn't been able to locate him, and the situation had only gotten exponentially worse. Murder had given way to public safety. We were certain that Hardaway was involved somehow and that he was extremely dangerous.

The morning news shows came on. Hardaway's face was the lead story on all three networks. It was like some nerve-racking doomsday countdown straight out of a disaster movie, only much worse. The thought that any minute in our city a bomb could go off or a poison be spread, maybe even by plane.

By seven, a few of the inevitable Hardaway sightings had started to trickle in. A clerk was sure he'd seen him in Oakland at an all-night market two weeks ago. Other calls came from Spokane, Albuquerque, even New Hampshire. Who knew if any of them were for real? But all the calls had to be checked out.

Molinari was on the phone with someone named Ronald Kull, from the WTO.

"I think we should issue some kind of communiqué," the deputy director pressed. "No admissions, but say that the organization is considering the grievances, if they show a cessation of violence. It'll buy us time. It could save lives. Maybe a lot of lives."

He seemed to have gotten some agreement and said he would draft the language. But then it had to be approved, by Washington and by the WTO.

All this red tape. The clock ticking. Some kind of disaster about to strike at any moment.

Then, like the e-mail foretold, it happened.

At 8:42 A.M. I don't think I'll ever forget the time of day.

Chapter 79

Kids had been drinking from a water foun-
tain at the Redwood City Elementary
School. They got sick. ... Those were the
first chilling words that we heard.

Every heart in the room slammed to a
stop at the same time. 8:42. Within seconds,
Molinari was patched through to the principal of the school. A decision was made to
evacuate it immediately. Claire, who had
strapped on a headset, was trying to get
through to the EMS vehicle carrying the kids
who had gotten sick.

Never before had I seen the most capable
people in the city so utterly panicked. Moli-

nari carefully instructed the principal: "No one touches the water until we get there. The school has to be cleared right now."

He ordered an FBI team on a copter down to Redwood City. The toxicology expert was hooked right into our speakers. "If it's ricin," he said, "we're going to see immediate convulsions, massive broncho-constriction, with intense, influenza-like symptoms."

Claire had gotten patched through to the school nurse. She identified herself and said, "I need you to carefully describe the symptoms the children are showing."

"I didn't know what it was," a frantic voice came back. "The kids were suddenly weak, showing signs of severe nausea. Temperatures were almost a hundred and four. Abdominal pain, throwing up."

One of the emergency copters had already gotten to the school and was circling, relaying film from above. Children were rushing out of the exits, guided by teachers. Frantic parents were arriving on the scene.

All of a sudden, a second report crackled over the airwaves. A worker had collapsed at a construction site in San Leandro. That was on the other side of the bay. They didn't know if it was a heart attack, or something ingested.

As we tried to follow up, a news flash broadcast came over one of the monitors: "Breaking news . . . In Redwood City, the local elementary school has been evacuated after children were rushed to a nearby hospital, having collapsed, showing signs of violent sickness, possibly related to a toxic substance. This, on top of broadcast alerts of possible terrorist activity today . . ."

"Any more reports of illness from the school?" Molinari spoke into the phone.

"None yet," the principal replied. The school was completely evacuated. The helicopter was still circling.

Suddenly a doctor from the ER gave us an update. "Their temperatures are one oh three point five to one oh four," the doctor reported. "Acute nausea and dyspnea. I don't know what's causing it. I've never had experience with this sort of thing before."

"You need to take immediate mouth and nasal swabs to determine if they were exposed," the toxins expert was instructing. "And chest X-rays. Look for any kind of bilateral infiltrates."

Claire cut in. "How are the pulmonary functions? Breathing? Lung activity?"

Everyone waited anxiously. "They seem to be functioning," the doctor reported.

Claire grabbed Molinari's arm. "Listen, I don't know what's going on here, but I don't think this is ricin," she said.

"How can you be sure?"

Claire had the floor. "Ricin attacks through a necrosis of the vascular cells. I *saw* the results. The lungs would already be starting to degrade. Also, ricin has a four-to-eight-hour incubation period, does it not, Dr. Taub?" she asked the toxicology expert on the line.

The expert begrudgingly agreed.

"That means they would've had to have been exposed during the night. If the lungs are symptom-free, I don't think it has anything to do with that water. I don't know if this is some kind of staph attack, or strychnine. . . . I don't think it's ricin."

The minutes passed slowly as the doctors in Redwood City ran through the first series of diagnostic tests.

An EMS team was already on the scene in San Leandro. They reported that the construction worker there was having a heart attack and had been stabilized. "A heart attack," they repeated.

Minutes later, Redwood City reported back. A chest X-ray showed no deterioration of the lungs in any of the children. "The bloodwork showed traces of staphylococcal enterotoxin B."

I watched Claire's expression.

"What the hell does that mean?" Mayor Fiske demanded.

"It means they've got a severe staph infection," she said, exhaling. "It's serious, and it's contagious, but it's not ricin."

Chapter 80

The Rincon Center was full at noon. Hundreds of people chatting over lunch, scanning the sports pages, rushing around with bags from the Gap or Office Max. Just relaxing under the enormous plane of water that fell from the glittering roof.

The pianist was playing. Mariah Carey. "A hero comes along . . ." But no one seemed to notice the music or the player. Hell, he was awful.

Robert sat reading the paper, his heart beating wildly. No more room for talk or argument, he kept thinking. No more waiting for change. Today he'd make his own. God

knows, he was one of the disenfranchised.
In and out of VA hospitals. Made crazy by his
combat experience, then abandoned. That
was what had made him a radical.

He tapped the leather briefcase with his
shoes, just to make sure it was still there. He
was reminded of something he had seen on
TV, in a dramatization of the Civil War. A run-
away slave had been freed and then con-
scripted to fight for the North. He fought in
some of the bloodiest battles of the war.
After one, he happened to spot his old master, shell-shocked and wounded among the
Confederate prisoners. "Hello, massa," the
slave went up to him and said, "looks like
bottom rail's on top now."

And that's what Robert was thinking as he
panned the unsuspecting lawyers and
bankers slopping down their lunch. *Bottom
rail's on top now. . . .*

Across the crowd, the man Robert was
waiting for stepped into the concourse — the
man with the salt-and-pepper hair. His blood
came alive. He stood, wrapping his fingers
around the case handle, keeping his eyes
fixed on the man — his target for today.

This was the moment, he told himself,
when all the fancy speeches and vows and

homilies turn into deed. He tossed down his newspaper. The area around the fountain was jam-packed. He headed toward the piano.

Are you afraid to act? Are you afraid to set the wheel in motion?

No, Robert said, *I'm ready. I've been ready for years.*

He stopped and waited at the piano. The pianist started up a new tune, the Beatles: "Something." More of the white man's garbage.

Robert smiled at the young red-headed dude behind the keyboard. He took a bill out of his wallet and stuffed it in the bowl.

Thanks, man, the pianist nodded.

Robert nodded back, almost laughed at the false camaraderie, and rested his briefcase against a leg of the piano. He checked the progress of his target—thirty feet away—and casually kicked the briefcase underneath the piano. *Take that, you sons of bitches!*

Robert started to drift slowly toward the north entrance. *This is it, baby.* This is what he'd been waiting for. He fumbled through his pocket for the stolen cell phone. The target was only about fifteen feet away. Robert turned at the exit doors and took it all in.

The man with the salt-and-pepper hair stopped at the piano, just as the Professor said he would. He took a dollar bill out of his wallet. Behind him, the eighty-foot column of water splashed down from the ceiling.

Robert pushed through the doors, walked away from the building, and depressed two preassigned keys on the cell phone — G-8.

Then the whole world seemed to burst into smoke and flame, and Robert felt the most incredible satisfaction of his entire life. This was a war he *wanted* to fight in.

He never saw the flash, only the building wrenching in a rumble of concrete and glass, doors blowing out behind him.

Start the revolution, baby. . . . Robert smiled to himself. *Bottom rail's on top now.* . . .

Chapter 81

There was a loud shout in the Emergency Command Center. One of the guys manning the police frequency yanked off his headset. "A bomb just went off at the Rincon Center!"

I turned to Claire and felt the life deflate out of me. The Rincon Center was one of the city's most spectacular settings, in the heart of the Financial District, home to government agencies, business offices, and hundreds of apartments. This time of day, it would be jammed. How many people had just died?

I wasn't waiting around for police reports to call in the damage or casualties. I ran out of the Emergency Command Center with Claire a step behind. We hopped in her medical examiner's van. It took about fifteen minutes for us to race downtown and fight our way through the maze of traffic, fire vehicles, and bystanders crowded around the stricken area. Reports coming over the radio said the bomb had gone off in the atrium, where it would be busiest at noon.

We ditched the van at the corner of Beale and Folsom and started to run. We could see smoke rising from the Rincon a couple of blocks away. We had to go to the Steuart Street entrance, running past the Red Herring, Harbor Court Hotel, the Y.

"Lindsay, this is so bad, so bad," Claire moaned.

The first thing that hit me was the blunt cordite smell. The outside glass doors were completely blown away. People sat on the sidewalk, coughing, bleeding, slashed by exploding glass, expelling smoke out of their lungs. Survivors were still being evacuated left and right. That meant the worst was inside.

I took a deep breath. "Let's go. Be *careful,* Claire."

Everything was covered with hot black

soot. Smoke stabbed at my lungs. The police were trying to clear some space. Fire crews were dousing sporadic blazes.

Claire knelt next to a woman whose face was burned and who was shouting that she couldn't see. I pushed past them, farther in. A couple of bodies were crumpled in the center of the atrium near the Rain Column, which continued to pour water into a pond built into the floor. *What have these people done? Is this their idea of war?*

Experienced cops were barking into hand-held radios, but I saw younger ones just standing around, blinking back tears.

In the center of the atrium, my eye fell on a mangle of twisted wood and melted wire — the remains of what looked like a piano. I spotted Niko Magitakos from the Bomb Squad crouched next to it. He had a look on his face that I will never forget. Something terrible like this, you pray it will never come.

I pushed my way over to Niko.

"The blast site," he said, tossing a piece of charred wood in the piano pile. "Those bastards, those *bastards,* Lindsay. People were just having lunch here."

I was no bomb expert, but I could see a ring of devastation — benches, trees, burn smears—the location of the casualties blasted out from the center of the atrium.

"Two witnesses say they saw a well-dressed black male. He left a briefcase under the piano and then split. My guess, it's the same work as the Marina case. C-4, detonated electronically. Maybe by phone."

A woman in a Bomb Squad jacket came running up, holding what looked like a fragment from a blown-apart leather case.

"Mark it," Niko instructed her. "If we can find the handle, maybe there'll even be a print."

"Wait," I said as she started to walk away. What she had found was a wide leather strap, the piece that closed over the top of a briefcase and buckled into the clasp. Two gold letters were monogrammed into the strap. AS.

A sickening feeling rose up inside me. They were fucking with us. They were mocking us. I knew what the letters stood for, of course.

A.S. August Spies.

My cell phone went off and I grabbed it. Cindy was on the line.

"Are you there, Lindsay?" she asked. "Are you okay?"

"I'm here. What's up?"

"They took credit for the bombing," she told me. "Somebody called it in to the paper. The caller said he was August Spies. He said, 'Three more days, then watch out!' He said this was just practice."

Chapter 82

By late afternoon it finally caught up with me that I hadn't gotten even an hour's sleep for the second night in three days.

I also started to feel that I was missing something important about the case. I was sure of it.

I called Cindy and Claire together. I'd been so focused on finding Hardaway, I'd missed something else.

Claire had spent the day in the morgue with the grim task of trying to identify the victims of the Rincon Center blast. There were sixteen dead so far, and more to come, unfortunately. She agreed to meet for a few minutes across the street at Susie's, our familiar corner table.

The minute I hit the street on the way to Susie's, I could feel the anxiety, see it on faces. Claire and Cindy were waiting for me inside.

"The note about Jill is the key." I told them my latest theory as we sipped our tea.

"The note said she was part of the state," Claire said, looking puzzled.

"Not that one. Cindy's e-mail. It said, 'This one wasn't like the others. . . .'"

"This one was personal," Cindy finished it off.

"You're thinking Jill had some personal contact with this guy?" Claire blinked. "Like what?"

"I don't know what I'm thinking. Just that each of these victims was chosen precisely. None of the killings have been random. So what led them to Jill? They tracked her. They cased her home and picked her up. Lightower, Bengosian . . . Something tied Jill to the two of them."

"Maybe one of her cases?" Cindy shrugged. Claire seemed unconvinced.

There was a lull in the conversation. We

looked around. The silence brought us all to the same place. The empty seat at the table.

"It's so strange to be here," Claire said, letting out a breath, "to be doing this, without Jill. To be talking about her."

"Jill's gonna help us," I whispered.

I looked at both of them. A renewed sparkle was in their eyes.

"Okay," Claire said, nodding, "how?"

"We're going to look over her old cases," I said. "I'll try and get someone on Sinclair's staff to pitch in."

"And we're looking for what exactly?" Cindy narrowed her eyes.

"You got the e-mail. Something *personal*," I said. "Just like this case is for us. Look at the faces in here, and out on the street. Somebody has to stop these bastards, these murderers."

Chapter 83

Bennett Sinclair hooked me up with Wendy Hong, a young prosecutor in his department, and with April, Jill's assistant. We requisitioned Jill's casework over the past eight years. All of it!

It was a mountain of paperwork, wheeled up from the law morgue in large laundry-style pushcarts and stacked in Jill's office in columns of thick, bound files.

So we started in.

By day, I still ran the investigation, trying to close in on Hardaway. But at night, and every other available moment I could find, I went downstairs and plowed through the files. Claire pitched in. So did Cindy. Deep into the night, it seemed Jill's light was the only one left on in the Hall.

This one was personal. The phrase rang in our ears.

But we didn't find anything. A lot of people's time wasted. If there was a connection to August Spies in Jill's life, it wasn't in her files. Where was it? It had to be there somewhere.

Finally, we loaded the last of the files to go back to the morgue.

"Go home," Claire said to me, exhausted herself. "Get some sleep." She struggled up and pulled on her raincoat. She placed her hand on my shoulder and squeezed. "We'll find another way, Lindsay. We will."

Claire was right. I needed a good night's sleep more than anything in the world, other than a warm bath. I had staked so much on this.

I checked in with the office one more time, then, for the first time I could remember, packed up to head home for some sleep. I got in the Explorer and started heading down Brannan for Potrero. I stopped at a light. I was feeling totally empty.

The light changed. I sat there. I knew inside that I wasn't going home.

I jerked a right when the light changed, and headed out on Sixteenth toward Buena Vista Park. It wasn't as if any brilliant idea flashed into my brain. . . . More like a lack of anything else to do.

Something connected them. I was sure of that much. I just hadn't found it.

There was a single patrol guy guarding Jill's town house when I pulled up. Crime scene tape blocked the stairs to the landing.

I ID'd myself to the young officer at the door, who was probably happy for the diversion at this time of night. I stepped inside Jill's house.

Chapter 84

A really creepy feeling came over me that this might not be something I should be doing. Walking around the home I had been to so many times, knowing Jill was dead. Seeing her things: a Burberry umbrella, Otis's food bowl, a stack of recent newspapers. I was overcome with a sense of loneliness, missing her more than ever.

I went into the kitchen. I leafed through some loose things on an old pine desk. Everything was just as she'd left it. A note to Ingrid, her housekeeper. A few bills. Jill's familiar handwriting. It was almost as if she were still there.

I went upstairs. I walked down the hall to Jill's study. This was where she did her work, spent a lot of her time. Jill's space.

I sat down at her desk. I smelled her scent. Jill had an old brass lamp. I flicked it on. Some letters scattered on the desk. One from her sister, Beth. Some photos: her and Steve and Otis at Moab.

What are you doing in here, Lindsay? I asked myself again. *What are you hoping to find? Something signed by August Spies? Don't be a fool.*

I opened one of the desk drawers. Files. Household things. Trips, airline mileage statements.

I got up and stepped over to the bookshelf. *The Voyage of the Narwhal, The Corrections,* stories by Eudora Welty. Jill always had good taste in books. Never knew when she found the time to read these things. But somehow she did.

I bent down and opened a cupboard under the shelf. I came upon boxes of old pictures. Trips taken, her sister's wedding. Some went back as far as her college graduation.

Look at Jill: frizzy hair, thin as a rail, but strong. They made me smile. I sat on the hardwood floor and leafed through them. *God, I miss you.*

I saw this old accordion-style folder, wrapped tightly by an elastic cord. I opened it. Lots of old things. What it contained surprised me. Letters, photos, newspaper clippings. Some report cards from when Jill was in high school. Her parents' wedding invitation.

And a file stuffed with newspaper clippings. I leafed through them. They were mostly about her father.

Her dad was a prosecutor, here and back in Texas. Jill told me he used to call her his little Second Chair. He'd died just a few months before, and it was clear how much Jill missed him. Most of the articles were on cases he had worked on or appointments he had received.

I came upon an old yellowed article. The source surprised me.

San Francisco Examiner. September 17, 1970.

The headline read PROSECUTOR NAMED IN BNA BOMBING CASE.

The Black National Army. The BNA was a radical group back in the sixties. Known for violent robberies and armed assaults.

I scanned the article. The prosecutor's name sent a chill racing down my back.

Robert Meyer.

Jill's father.

Chapter 85

An hour later I was stabbing at Cindy's front doorbell. Two-thirty in the morning. I heard the locks turn, and the door slowly cracked open. Cindy was staring at me in a long Niners shirt, bleary-eyed. I had probably woken her out of her best sleep in three days.

"This better be good," she said as she flipped the lock.

"It's good, Cindy." I shoved the old *Examiner* article in front of her face. "I think I found out how Jill's connected to the case."

Fifteen minutes later we were bouncing along the darkened, empty streets of the city in my Explorer, down to the *Chronicle*'s office on Fifth and Mission.

"I didn't even know Jill's father worked out here," Cindy said, then yawned.

"He started here, out of law school, before he moved back to Texas. Right after Jill was born."

We got to her cubicle at about three A.M. The lights in the newsroom were dimmed, a couple of young stringers manning the overnight wires, caught playing video bridge.

"Overnight efficiency audit," Cindy said to them, straight- faced. "You guys just failed."

She wheeled herself in front of her screen and fired up the computer. She plugged a few search words into the *Chronicle*'s database: *Robert Meyer. BNA.* Then she slapped the ENTER key.

Several matches popped up on the screen right away. We plowed through a lot of unrelated articles of antiwar and BNA activity in the sixties. Then we found something.

PROSECUTOR NAMED IN DEADLY BNA RAID CASE.

A series of articles from September 1970.

We scrolled back from there, and bingo!

FEDS, POLICE RAID BNA STRONGHOLD. FOUR DEAD IN SHOOTOUT.

It was in the days of the sixties radicals. Constant protests over the war, SDS riots on Sproul Plaza in Berkeley. We scrolled through several articles. The BNA had robbed a few banks and then a Brink's truck. A guard, a hostage, and two cops were killed in the robbery. Two BNA members were on the FBI's list of Top Ten Most Wanted Fugitives.

We scrolled through whatever the *Chronicle* had on file. A BNA hideout was raided the night of December 6, 1969. The Feds had surrounded a house on a quiet street in Berkeley based on a tip from a CI. They came in, guns blazing.

Five radicals in the house were killed. Among the dead were Fred Whitehouse, a leader of the group, and two women.

There was one white kid shot dead in the raid, a student at Berkeley. From an upper-middle-class background near Sacramento. Family and friends insisted he didn't even know how to fire a gun. Just an idealistic kid caught up protesting an immoral war.

No one would say what he was doing in the house.

William "Billy" Danko was his name.

Chapter 86

A grand jury was convened to investigate the shootings at the BNA hideout. Nasty charges were hurled left and right. The case was given to a rising prosecutor in the D.A.'s office. Robert Meyer. Jill's father.

The jury at the trial found no evidence of any police misconduct. Those who were killed, the police argued, were among the FBI's most wanted, though the description seemed a stretch for Billy Danko. Federal agents paraded a cache of guns confiscated in the raid: Uzis, grenade launchers, piles of ammo. A gun was found in Fred Whitehouse's hand—though sympathizers claimed it had been planted.

"Okay," Cindy said wearily, and pushed back from the screen, "where do we go from here?"

The database referred to an article from 1971, a year later, in the *Chronicle*'s Sunday news magazine.

"You got a morgue downstairs, don't you?"

"Yes, we do. Downstairs. A morgue."

It was now close to four A.M. We flicked on a light in the morgue, and there was nothing but row after row of metal shelves filled with mesh and wire bins.

I frowned, deflated. "You know the system, Cindy?"

"Of course I know the system," she replied. "You come in here during normal working hours and you ask the guy sitting at the desk."

We split up and roamed the dark, crammed corridors. Cindy wasn't exactly sure if the files went back that far; what we were searching for might only be on film.

Finally I heard her shout, "I found something!"

I wound my way through the dark rows,

following the sound of her voice. When I found Cindy, she was hauling down bundled old issues of the magazine supplement in large plastic bins. They were labeled by year.

We sat on the cold, concrete floor, side by side, barely enough light to read by.

Still, we quickly found the article the database had referred us to. It was an exposé titled "What Really Happened to the Hope Street Five."

According to the writer, the local police had fabricated the whole crime scene to get rid of the insurgents. They had been tipped off by an unnamed CI. It was a massacre, not an arrest. Supposedly the victims were sleeping in their beds.

A lot of the article was focused on the white victim in the raid, Billy Danko. The FBI had claimed he was a Weatherman and tied him to a bombing at a regional office of Raytheon, a manufacturer of weapons. The article in the *Chronicle* contradicted most of the FBI's facts about Danko, who did seem to be an innocent victim.

It was four in the morning. I was getting frustrated, angry.

Cindy and I seemed to fix on it at the same time.

The court proceedings. It was brought out that the BNA and the Weathermen used code names when they contacted one another. Fred Whitehouse was Bobby Z, after a Black Panther who was gunned down. Leon Mickens was Vlad—Vladimir Ilyich Lenin. Joanne Crow was Sasha, a woman who had blown herself up fighting the junta in Chile.

"You see it, Cindy?" I looked at her in the thinning light.

The name that Billy Danko had chosen for himself was August Spies.

Jill had shown us the way.

Chapter 87

The lights were blazing in Molinari's office —
the only lights on in the Hall at six A.M.

He was on the phone when I went in. His
face brightened into what I took as a worn
smile, pleased but exhausted. No one was
getting any sleep these days.

"I was just trying to assure the chief of
staff," he said, signing off the phone and smiling, "that we weren't the security equal out
here of, say, Chechnya — with larger bridges.
Tell me you have something, anything."

I pushed across the yellowed, folded article I had found in Jill's study.

Molinari picked up the article, PROSECUTOR NAMED IN BNA BOMBING CASE. He scanned it.

"What was it you called them, Joe? Radicals from the sixties who you said are still out there, who never surfaced?"

"White rabbits?" he said.

"What if it wasn't political? What if there was something else motivating them? Or maybe it's partly political, but there's something else?"

"Motivating *what*, Lindsay?"

I pushed across the last article, the Sunday magazine supplement, folded to the part about Billy Danko's code name, circled in bright red: August Spies.

"To get back in the game. To commit these murders. Maybe to get some kind of revenge. I don't know everything yet. There's something here, though."

For the next few minutes I briefed Molinari on everything that we had—right up to the prosecutor Robert Meyer, Jill's father.

Molinari blinked glassily. He looked at me as if I might be crazy. And it sounded crazy. Whatever I had was flying in the face of the investigation, the pronouncements of the killers, the wisdom of every law-enforcement agency in the country.

"Just where do you want to go with this, Lindsay?" Molinari finally asked.

"We've got to find out whatever we can about the people in that house. I'd start with Billy Danko. His family was from Sacramento. The FBI has files on what happened, right? Department of Justice, whatever it is. I need to know everything the Feds know."

Molinari shook his head slowly back and forth. I realized I was asking for a lot. He closed his eyes for a second and leaned back in his chair. When he opened them I saw the faintest outline of a smile. "I knew there was a reason I missed you, Lindsay."

I took that as a yes.

"What I didn't know" — he pushed back his chair — "was that it was due to the likely prospect we're both going to have some time on our hands after we're removed from our jobs."

"I missed you, too," I said.

Chapter 88

San Francisco was in a panic the likes of which I had never seen before. The news stories never seemed to stop. Meanwhile, where the hell were we? Not close enough to the killers, I was afraid.

My whole theory depended on finding some way to make the other victims fit in with the current murders. I was certain there was a connection.

Bengosian was from Chicago. That seemed a long shot to tie in. But I remembered Lightower had gone to Berkeley. His CLO had told us that when we were up at Lightower's company after he was killed.

I placed a call to Dianne Aronoff, Mort Lightower's sister, and caught her at home. We talked and I found out that her brother had been a member of the SDS. In '69, his junior year at Berkeley, he had taken a leave of absence.

Nineteen sixty-nine was the year of the Hope Street raid. Did that mean anything? It just might.

About one o'clock, Jacobi knocked on my window. "I think we found your guy Danko's father."

He and Cappy had started with the phone book, then matched up the address with a local high school. Danko's father was still in Sacramento. Same address as they had lived in back in 1969. A man had answered when Cappy called. Hung up as soon as the inspectors had brought up Billy Danko's name.

"There's an FBI office down there." Jacobi shrugged. "Or?"

"Here"—I jumped up, flipping him the keys to the Explorer—"you drive."

Chapter 89

It was about two hours on Highway 80 any way you cut it to Sacramento, and we kept the Explorer at a steady seventy-five over the Bay Bridge. An hour and fifty minutes later we pulled up in front of a slightly run-down fifties-style ranch. We needed a win here, needed it badly.

The house was large but neglected, a slope of faded lawn and a fenced-in lot in back. Danko's father was a doctor, I recalled. Thirty years ago, this might've been one of the nicest houses on the block.

I took off my sunglasses and knocked on

the front door. It took a while for someone to answer, and I was feeling impatient, to say the least.

Finally an old man opened and peered out at us. I could see his nose and sharp, pointed chin — a resemblance to the picture of Billy Danko in the *Chronicle* magazine.

"You the idiots who called on the phone?" He stood there, regarding us warily. "Of course you are."

"I'm Lieutenant Lindsay Boxer," I said. "And this is Homicide Inspector Warren Jacobi. Do you mind if we come in?"

"I mind," he said, but he swung the screen door open anyway. "I've got nothing to say to the police if it concerns my son, other than accepting their full apology for his murder."

He led us back through musty, paint-chipped halls into a small den. It didn't seem that anyone else was living with him.

"We were hoping to ask you just a few questions regarding your son," Jacobi said.

"Ask." Danko sank himself into a patchwork couch. "Better time to ask questions was thirty years ago. William was a good boy, a *great* boy. We raised him to think for himself, and he did, made choices of conscience—the right ones, it was proven out later. Losing that boy cost me everything I had. My wife . . ." He nodded toward a black-and-white portrait of a middle-aged woman. "Everything."

"We're sorry for what happened." I sat on the edge of a badly stained armchair. "No one's here to cause you more distress. I'm sure you're familiar with what's been going on in San Francisco recently. A lot of people have died there."

Danko shook his head. "Thirty years later, and you still won't let him rest in peace."

I glanced at Jacobi. This was going to be a tough go. I started in talking about Jill, how we had found the connection between her father and the raid on the Hope Street house. Then how one of the other victims, Lightower, also had a connection to Berkeley and the student revolts.

"Don't mean to tell you your job, *Inspectors*"—Carl Danko smiled—"but that sounds like a lot of crazy suppositions to me."

"Your son had a code name," I said, "August Spies. August Spies is the name that's being used by the people who are doing these killings."

Carl Danko snorted derisively and reached for a pipe. He seemed to find all of this humorous.

"Do you know anyone who might be involved?" I pressed. "One of Billy's friends? Maybe someone's been in touch with you lately?"

"Whoever is doing it, God bless him." Carl Danko cleaned out his pipe. "Truth is, you've wasted your time coming out here. I can't help you a lick. And if I could . . . I hope somehow you can understand why I might not be so disposed to help the San Francisco Police. Now please leave my house."

Jacobi and I stood up. I took a step toward the door, praying for some kind of epiphany before I got there. I stopped at the picture of his wife. Then I noticed a photo next to hers.

It was a family shot.

Something caused me to focus on the faces.

There was another son in the photo.

Younger. Maybe sixteen. A spitting image of his mother. The four of them smiling, not a care on what seemed a pleasant, sunny day in the distant past.

"You have another son." I turned back to Danko.

"Charles . . ." He shrugged.

I picked up the photo. "Maybe we should talk to him. He might know something."

"Doubt it." Danko stared at me. "He's dead, too."

Chapter 90

Back in the Explorer, I called in to Cappy. "I want you to run the background on a Charles Danko. Born in Sacramento, 1953–54. Possibly deceased. That's the best I have. And go back as far as you have to go. If this guy's dead, I want to see the death certificate to prove it."

"I'll get on it," Cappy said. "Meanwhile, I got one for you. George Bengosian, Lieutenant. You were right, he did get a pre-med degree from the University of Chicago. But that was *after* he transferred there from Berkeley. Bengosian was there in 'sixty-nine."

"Thanks, Cappy. Great work. Keep it up."

So now we had three—Jill, Lightower, and Bengosian—who were tied to the murderous police raid on Hope Street. And the code name August Spies linked to Billy Danko.

I didn't know what to do with it yet. As Danko said, it was all a bunch of suppositions.

While Jacobi drove back to the city, I finally dozed for a bit. It was my first solid sleep in three days. We got back to the Hall about six. "In case you were wondering," Jacobi said, "you snore."

"Purr," I corrected. "I purr."

Before heading back to my office, I wanted to check on Molinari. I ran upstairs and squeezed myself into his office. A meeting was in progress. What was this?

Chief Tracchio was sitting at his desk. So was Tom Roach from the FBI. And Strickland, who was in charge of the G-8 advance security.

"Lightower was there," I announced, barely able to hold back my excitement. "At Berkeley—at the time of the BNA raid. George Bengosian was, too. They were all there."

"I know," Molinari said.

Chapter 91

It only took me a second. "You found the FBI file on the BNA?"

"Better," Molinari said. "We found one of the FBI agents who was in charge of the raid on Hope Street.

"William Danko *was* a card-carrying member of the Weathermen. You can be sure of it. He was sighted casing the site of the regional offices of Grumman, which were bombed in September of 1969. His code name, August Spies, was picked up in monitored phone traffic of known Weathermen lines. The kid was no innocent, Lindsay. He was involved in murder."

Molinari pushed forward a yellow legal pad filled with his handwriting. "The FBI had begun following him about three months before the raid. There were a couple of others involved out of the Berkeley cell. The FBI was able to turn one of them, use him as a CI. It's amazing how the threat of twenty-five years in a federal prison puts a crimp in a promising medical career."

"Bengosian!" I said. A rush surged through my veins. I felt validated.

Molinari nodded. "They turned Bengosian, Lindsay. That's how they got to the house on Hope Street that night. Bengosian betrayed his friends. You were right—and there's more."

"Lightower," I said expectantly.

"He was Danko's roommate," Molinari replied. "The school cracked down on students active in the SDS. Maybe Lightower decided it was time for a semester abroad.

"And one of the FBI agents who led the raid, who went inside the house that morning, he got promoted. Spent his twenty years in the Bureau, retired right here in San Francisco. His name was Frank T. Seymour. Name ring a bell?"

Yeah, it rang a bell, but it didn't fill me with exhilaration. Just a sickening feeling.

Frank T. Seymour was one of the people killed in the blast at the Rincon Center.

Chapter 92

It was night now and Michelle liked the night. She could watch the *Simpsons,* reruns of *Friends*. Laugh a bit, like before everything had started, like when she was a kid in Eau Claire.

They'd had to ditch the Oakland apartment where they had lived for the past six months. Now they'd moved into Julia's house in the Berkeley flats.

And they couldn't go out much anymore. The situation was too tight. Sometimes on TV she saw a photograph of Mal, except the news reports called him Stephen Hardaway. Robert had moved in, too. It was the four of them now. And maybe Charles Danko would show up soon, too. Supposedly, he had the final plans, the endgame, which Mal promised would blow everybody's mind. It was *huge.*

Michelle turned off the TV and went downstairs. Mal was hunched over the wires, tinkering with the new device, the latest bomb. There was a plan, he said, how they were gonna get this baby inside. Just being in the same place with the damn thing freaked her out.

She crept up behind him. "Mal, you want something to eat? I can fix you something."

"You can see I'm working, Michelle." More of a snap than a reply. He was soldering a red wire into a wooden table leg that she knew encased the blasting cap.

She put a hand on his shoulder. "I need to talk with you, Mal. I think I want to leave."

Mal stiffened up from the bomb. He pulled the lenses off his head, wiped the sweaty hair off of his face.

"You're going to leave?" Mal said, nodding in her face, as if he found this amusing. "And you're going where? Hop on a bus and go home? Back to Geewhizconsin? Enroll in Geewhizconsin junior college, after blowing up a couple of kids in the big city?"

Tears started in Michelle's eyes. Telltale signs of weakness, she knew. Dreaded sentimentality.

"Stop it, Mal."

"You're a wanted *killer,* honey. The cute little nanny who blew up her kids. Did that slip your mind?"

Suddenly she saw it clearly. Lots of things. That even if they did this job, this last one, Mal would never go away with her. When she closed her eyes at night she could see the Lightower kids. Sitting around at breakfast. Getting dressed for school. She knew she had done terrible things. No matter how much she wished otherwise, Mal was right, there was nowhere for her to go. She was the murderous au pair. She always would be.

"Now come on," Mal said, suddenly gentler. "As long as you're here, you can help me, baby. I need that pretty finger of yours. On that wire. You remember, nothing to worry about."

He held up the phone. "No juice, no boost, right? We're gonna be heroes, Michelle. We're gonna save the world from the bad guys. They're never ever going to forget us."

Chapter 93

One A.M., but who could sleep?

Molinari came into the squad room. I was watching the wires with Paul Chin. He looked at me and sighed. "Charles Danko."

He tossed a green folder on the desk across from me. It was marked PRIVILEGED INFORMATION, FBI. "They had to go deep in the cold files to find him."

I felt my blood rush. My skin prickled. Did this mean we were close to finding him?

"He went to the University of Michigan," Molinari said. "Arrested twice for disorderly conduct and inciting to riot. Picked up in New York in 1973 for illegal possession of firearms. A town house he lived in there just blew up one afternoon. Here one minute, gone the next."

"Sure sounds like our boy."

"He was being sought in connection with a bombing of the Pentagon in 1972. An expert in explosives. After that town house blew in New York, he disappeared. No one knew whether he was in the country or out. Charles Danko's simply been missing for thirty years. No one's even chasing him."

"A white rabbit," I said.

He laid out an old rap sheet dated 1974 and a faxed black-and-white FBI wanted poster. On it was a slightly older version of the boyish face I had seen in the family photo at the Danko house.

"There's our man," Molinari said. "Now how the hell do we find him?"

Chapter 94

"Lieutenant!" I heard a loud knocking on my glass.

I bolted up. My watch read 6:30 A.M. I must have dozed off waiting for Molinari to report with more news on Danko.

Paul Chin was at my door. "Lieutenant, you better get on line three. *Now . . ."*

"Danko?" I blinked myself awake.

"Better. We got a woman from Wisconsin who thinks her daughter is tied up with Stephen Hardaway. I think she knows where she is!"

In the seconds it took to knock the sleep out of my brain, Chin went back to his desk and got a backup recording going. I picked up the phone.

"Lieutenant Lindsay Boxer," I cleared my throat and said.

The woman started in as if she had left off in mid-sentence with Chin, her voice upset, maybe not too educated. Midwestern.

"I always told her something with this smart-ass guy didn't add up. She said he was so brilliant. *Brilliant,* my ass . . . She always wanted to do good, my Michelle. She was easy to take advantage of. I said, 'Just go to the state school. You can be anything you want.'"

"Your daughter's name is Michelle?" I picked up a pen. "Ms. . . . ?"

"Fontieul. That's right, Michelle Fontieul."

I scribbled down the name. "Why don't you just tell me what you know?"

"I seen him, you know," the woman recounted. "That fellow on TV. The one everybody's looking for. My Michelle's hooked up with him.

"Course his name wasn't Stephen then. What'd she call him on the phone? Malcolm? Mal. They drove through here heading out west. I think he was from Portland or Washington. He got her into this 'protesting' thing. I didn't even understand half of what it meant. I tried to warn her."

"You're sure this was the same man you saw on TV?" I pressed.

"I'm sure. Course, his hair's different now. And he didn't have no beard. I knew—"

I interrupted. "When was the last time you spoke to your daughter, Ms. Fontieul?"

"I don't know, maybe three months. *She* always called. She'd never leave her numbers. This last time, though, she sounded a little strange. She said she was really doing some good for once. She comes out and tells me that I raised her well. That she loved me. I was thinking, maybe she'd got herself knocked up is all."

All this matched. What we knew about Hardaway and the description we'd gotten from the owner of the KGB Bar. "Do you have any way to contact your daughter? An address?"

"I had some address, I think it was maybe a friend's. I got this P.O. box. Michelle said I could always send something there if I needed to. Box three-three-three-eight. Care of Mail Boxes, Etc., on Broad Street, Oakland, California."

I glanced at Chin, both of us scribbling at

the same time. The place wouldn't open up for a couple of hours. We'd have to get the FBI out to her in Wisconsin. Get a photo of her daughter. In the meantime, I asked if she would describe her to me.

"Blond. Blue eyes." The woman hesitated. "Michelle was always pretty, I'll grant her that. I don't know if I'm doing the right thing. She's just a kid, Lieutenant."

I thanked her for coming forward. And I told her I'd make sure her daughter was treated fairly, if she was mixed up in this, which I had no doubt she was.

"I'm going to put you on with another officer," I told her, "but before I do, I need to ask you one more thing." A thought had crept into my head, going back to that first day. "Did your daughter have any breathing ailments?"

"Why, yes," she said, pausing, "she always did have asthma, Lieutenant. Been carrying around a puffer since she was ten years old."

I looked at Chin through the glass. "I think we just found Wendy Raymore."

Chapter 95

Cindy Thomas headed into work on the Market Street bus, same as every morning, but that day with the gnawing premonition that something was going to break soon. One way or the other. August Spies had promised as much.

The BART was crowded this morning, standing room only. It took two stops for her even to find a seat. She took out her *Chronicle* as she did every morning and scanned page one. A shot of Mayor Fiske, flanked by Deputy Director Molinari and Tracchio. The G-8 meetings were still a go. Her story, on the possible link to Billy Danko, was the right-hand column above the fold.

A girl with cropped, dyed red hair in overalls and a crocheted sweater moved close by. Cindy looked up; something about her struck her as familiar. The girl had three earrings in her left ear and a barrette in the shape of a sixties peace symbol in her hair. Pretty, in a waiflike way.

Cindy kept one eye on the route, which she knew just from the stores on Market Street. The man next to her got up at Van Ness.

The girl in the overalls squeezed into the seat beside her. Cindy smiled and turned the page. More articles on the G-8 thing. The girl in the overalls seemed to be reading over her shoulder.

Then she met Cindy's eyes. "They're not going to stop, you know."

Cindy smiled halfheartedly; conversation wasn't something she needed before eight A.M. This time the girl wouldn't let her gaze go.

"They're not going to stop, Miss Thomas. *I did try.* I did like you said, and tried."

Cindy froze. Everything inside her seemed to come to a stop.

She looked into the girl's face. She was older than she had seemed — maybe mid-twenties. Cindy thought to ask how she knew her name, but then in that same instant, it all came clear.

This was the person she'd been talking to on the Internet. This was the girl who had a hand in killing Jill. Possibly, the au pair.

"Listen to me. I snuck out, they don't know I'm here. Something terrible is going to happen," the girl said. "At the G-8 meeting. Another bomb. Or *worse*. I don't know exactly where, but it's gonna be big, the biggest one. A lot of people will die. Now *you* try to stop it."

Every muscle in Cindy's body tensed. She didn't know what she should do. Grab her, shout, stop the bus? Every law-enforcement agent in town was looking for this girl. But something held Cindy back. "Why are you telling me this?" she asked.

"I'm sorry, Miss Thomas." The girl touched Cindy's arm. "I'm sorry about all of them, Eric, Caitlin. That lawyer, your friend. I know we've done some terrible things. . . . I wish I could undo them. I can't."

"You've got to turn yourself in." Cindy

stared at her. She glanced around, petrified that one of the other passengers would hear. "It's over. They know who you are."

"I have something for you." The girl ignored her pleas. She pressed a folded-up piece of paper into Cindy's hand. "I don't know any way to stop it now. Except this. It's better if I stay with them. Just in case the plans change."

The bus came to a stop at the Metro Civic Center. Cindy unfolded the paper the girl had given her.

She read: *722 Seventh Street Berkeley.*

"Oh my God," Cindy gasped. The girl was telling her where they were hiding.

Suddenly the girl was standing up, heading for the exit. The rear door hissed open.

"You can't go back there!" Cindy hollered.

The girl turned, but she kept walking.

"Wait!" she shouted. "Don't go back there."

The girl seemed surprised, and lost. She hesitated for a second. "I'm sorry," she mouthed. "I need to do it this way." Then she hurried off the bus.

Cindy leaped up as the doors closed, yanking the cord, shouting to the driver to open them again. It was an emergency! By the time she jumped out onto the platform, Michelle Fontieul had disappeared into the early-morning crowd.

Cindy got on the phone to Lindsay. "I know where they are! I have an address."

Part Five

Chapter 96

The largest assault team in the city's history was building up around the run-down white house at 722 Seventh Street in Berkeley. San Francisco SWAT details, Berkeley and Oakland contingents, federal agents from the FBI and the DHS.

The area was completely blocked off from traffic. Neighboring houses were quietly cleared one by one. The Bomb Squad was readied. EMS vans were pulled into place.

A gray Chevy van had pulled into the driveway twenty minutes earlier. Somebody was home.

I was able to station myself close to Molinari, who was in phone contact with Washington. A Special Operations captain, Joe Szerbiak, was in charge of the assault team.

"Here's what we do," Molinari said, kneeling behind the barricade of a black patrol car maybe thirty yards away from the house. "We make one call. Give them a chance to surrender. If they don't"—he nodded to Szerbiak—"it's yours."

The plan was to shoot in tear gas canisters and force whoever was in the house out. If they came out *cool,* meaning voluntarily, we would force them to the ground, pick them up.

"And if they come out *hot?*" Joe Szerbiak asked, putting on his bulletproof vest.

Molinari shrugged. "If they come out shooting, we have to take them down."

The wild card in the siege was the explosives. We knew they had bombs. What had taken place at the Rincon Center two days before was in the front of everybody's mind.

The assault team was readied. Several marksmen were in place. The team that was going in assembled inside an armored van, ready to swing into place. Cindy Thomas was with us. A girl inside seemed to trust her. Michelle. Who might be Wendy Raymore, the au pair.

I was nervous and agitated. I wanted this over. No more bloodshed, just over.

"You think they know we're out here?" Tracchio surveyed the house from behind the hood of a radio car.

"If they don't," Molinari said, "they're about to." He looked at Szerbiak. "Captain," he said with a nod, "you can make that call."

Chapter 97

Inside 722 Seventh Street, everyone and everything was going crazy.

Robert, the vet, had grabbed an automatic rifle and was crouched below one of the front windows, sizing up the scene outside. "There's an army out there! Cops everywhere I look!"

Julia was screaming and acting like a crazy woman. "I told you to get out of my house! I told you to get out!" She looked toward Mal. "What are we going to do now? *What are we going to do?*"

Mal seemed calm. He went over to the window, peeked through the curtains. Then he headed into the other room and came back wheeling a black case. "Probably die," he answered.

Michelle's heart seemed to be beating a thousand beats per second. Any moment, armed, uniformed men could burst in. Part of her was gripped with fear, part was ashamed. She knew she had let down her friends. Ended everything they had fought for. But she had helped murder women and children, and now maybe she could stop the killing.

Suddenly the phone rang. For a second everyone turned, eyes fixed on the phone. The rings were like alarm bells going off.

"Pick it up," Robert said to Mal. "You want to be the leader. Pick it up."

Mal walked over. Four, five rings. Finally he lifted the phone.

He listened for a second. His face didn't register fear or surprise. He even told them his name. "Stephen Hardaway," he said proudly.

Then he listened for a long time. "I hear you," he answered. He put down the receiver, swallowed, and looked around. "They say we have this one chance. Anyone who wants to leave, you'd better go now."

The room was deathly quiet. Robert at the

window. Julia, her back pressed up against the wall. Mal, finally seeming shocked and out of answers. Michelle wanted to cry that she had brought this upon them.

"Well, they ain't putting their hands on me," Robert said. He picked up his automatic rifle, his back to the kitchen door, eyeing the van parked in the driveway.

He winked, a sort of silent farewell. Then he yanked open the door and ran out of the house.

About four feet from the van he raised the gun, squeezing off a long burst in the direction of the police. There were two loud cracks. Just two. Robert stopped in his tracks. He spun around, a surprised look on his face, crimson stains widening on his chest.

"Robert!" Julia screamed. She smashed the barrel of her gun through the front window and started shooting wildly. Then she was hurled backward and didn't move again.

Suddenly a black canister sailed through the front window. Gas started to leak out. Then another black canister. A stinging, bitter cloud began to envelop the room, clawing at Michelle's lungs.

"Oh, Mal," she cried. She looked toward

him. He was standing there, no fear on his face now.

In his hands he held a portable phone.

"I'm not going out there," he said.

"I'm not, either." She shook her head.

"You really are a brave little girl." Mal smiled.

She watched him punch in a four-digit number. A second later she heard a ring. It came from the suitcase.

Then a second ring.

A third . . .

"Remember"—Mal took a breath—"no juice, no boost. Right, Michelle?"

Chapter 98

When the house blew we were crouched behind the cover of a black-and-white, barely a hundred feet away.

There were bold orange flashes as the windows exploded. Then the house seemed to lift off its foundation, a fiery cloud ripping the whole thing apart through the roof.

"Get down!" Molinari yelled. "Everybody down!"

The blast hurled us backward. I took Cindy, who'd been standing next to me, down to the ground, shielding her from the force of the blast and the shower of debris.

We lay there as the searing gust lifted over us. A few cries of "Holy shit" and "Are you all right?"

Slowly, we got back up. "Oh, God . . . ," Cindy groaned.

Where a second ago a white clapboard house had been standing, now there was only smoke, fire, and a crater of blown-out walls.

"Michelle," Cindy muttered. "Come on, Michelle."

We watched the fire rise as the wind whipped the flames. No one came out. No one could have lived through such a blast.

Sirens started up. Frantic radio transmissions filled the air. I heard cops shouting into walkie-talkies: "We have a major explosion at seven twenty-two Seventh Street. . . ."

"Maybe she wasn't in there." Cindy shook her head, still staring at the devastated house.

I put my arm around her. "They killed Jill, Cindy."

Later, after the fire crews had doused the blaze to smoking cinders and the EMS teams were going around tagging the charred remains, I sifted through the debris myself.

Was it over now? Was the threat gone? How many were in there? I didn't know. It looked like four or five. Hardaway was probably dead. Was Charles Danko in there, too? August Spies?

Claire had arrived. She was kneeling over the covered bodies, but the parts were burned almost beyond recognition.

"I'm looking for a white male," I told her, "about fifty."

"Best I can tell, there seem to be four of them," she said. "The black male who was shot in the driveway. Three others inside. Two of them female, Lindsay."

Joe Molinari came over to me. He'd been giving Washington an update on what had just happened. "You okay?" he asked.

"It's not over," I said, nodding at the tagged mounds.

"Danko?" He shrugged. "The medical people will have to tell us that. In any case, his network is gone, his cell. The device, too. What can he do now?"

Amid the wreckage, I spotted something—a barrette. There was something almost funny about it. I reached down and picked it up.

"Voice of the people be heard," I said to Molinari, holding out the barrette.

There was a peace symbol on it.

Chapter 99

Charles Danko was wandering the streets of San Francisco aimlessly and thinking about what had just happened in Berkeley, where his friends had died for the cause, died as martyrs just like William had a long time ago.

I could kill a lot of people right now. Right here.

He knew he could go on a rampage and they wouldn't catch him for several hours, maybe longer if he got his head screwed on straight, if he thought this through—if he was a careful killer.

You're dead, slick young business creep in

your expensive-looking black-on-black ensemble.

You're dead, too, blond fashionista.

You. And you. You! You! You four frolicking asshole buddies!

God, it would be so easy to let his rage out now.

The police, the FBI, they were pathetic at their job of "protecting" the people.

They had everything wrong, didn't they?

They didn't understand that this could be about justice *and* revenge. The two concepts were perfectly compatible; they could go hand in hand. He was following in his brother William's footsteps, honoring his fallen brother's inspired dream, and at the same time he was avenging William. Two causes were better than one. Twice the motivation; twice the anger.

The faces he was passing, the expensive clothes, the absurd shops, were all starting to blur before his eyes—all of them were guilty. The whole country was.

They didn't get it, though. Not yet.

The war was right here in their streets of gold—the war was here to stay.

No one could stop it anymore.

There would always be more soldiers.

After all, that's what he was, just a soldier.

He stopped at a pay phone and made two calls.

The first, to another soldier.

The second, to his mentor, the person who had thought of everything, including how to use him.

Charles Danko had made his decision: tomorrow was a go for terror.

Nothing had changed.

Chapter 100

The next day, the G-8 meetings were scheduled to begin as originally planned. The
hard-liners, the tough guys in Washington,
wanted it that way. So be it.

The proceedings were set for that night,
with a reception in the Rodin Gallery at the
Palace of the Legion of Honor overlooking
the Golden Gate Bridge.

It would be hosted by Eldridge Neal, one
of the most admired African Americans in
the country, the current vice president. Every
available uniform was assigned to security
detail at the venues and along the routes.
Every ID would be triple-checked, every

trash can and air vent sniffed by explosive-detecting dogs.

But Danko was still out there.

And Carl Danko was still the only link to his son I had.

I drove back to Sacramento while the rest of the department prepared for the G-8 festivities. Carl Danko seemed surprised to see me again. "Thought you'd be accepting some kind of Medal of Honor today. The killing of young kids seems to be a habit with you people. So, why are you here?"

"Your son," I told him.

"My son is *dead*."

But Danko sighed and let me in. I followed him back to his den. A fire was burning there. He knelt down and stoked the flames, then sat down in an easy chair.

"Like I told you before, the time to talk about William was thirty years ago."

"Not Billy," I said. *"Charles."*

Danko seemed to hesitate. "I told the federal boys—"

"We know," I interrupted him mid-sentence. "We know his record, Mr. Danko. We know he isn't dead."

The old man snarled, "You people won't stop, will you? First William, now Charlie. Go take your medals, Lieutenant. You caught your killers. What makes you think you can come in here and tell me Charlie is alive?"

"George Bengosian," I answered.

"Who?"

"George Bengosian. The second victim. He knew Billy back at Berkeley. More than knew him, Mr. Danko. He was the one who turned your son in."

Danko shifted in his easy chair. "What's that supposed to mean?"

"And Frank Seymour? He was killed in the Rincon Center blast the other day. Seymour was the lead agent on the Hope Street raid that killed your son. Charles is out there. He's killing innocent people, Mr. Danko. I think he's gone mad. I think you do, too."

The old man took a deep breath. He stared into the fire, then got up and went over to a desk. He took out a pack of letters from a bottom drawer. Tossed them in front of me on the coffee table.

"I didn't lie. My son *has* been dead to me. I've seen him once, five minutes on a Seattle street corner, in the past thirty years. Few years ago, these began to arrive. Once a year, around my birthday."

Jesus, I'd been right all along. Charles Danko was alive. . . .

I took the letters and began to sort through them.

The old man shrugged. "Guess he's teaching college or something."

I inspected the envelopes; no return addresses. But the last four had originated up north. Portland, Oregon. One, as recently as January 7, four months ago.

Portland.

A thought flashed through my head. It couldn't be a coincidence. Stephen Hardaway had gone to college in Portland. Reed. I looked back at the old man. "You say he's teaching? Teaching where?"

He shook his head. "Don't know."

But *I* knew. Suddenly I knew with a clarity that was inescapable.

Danko was at Reed, wasn't he? All this time, he was up there teaching college.

That was how he and Stephen Hardaway met.

Chapter 101

I was patched through to Molinari at the Palace of the Legion of Honor. The vice president's reception was less than two hours away. The G-8 had begun.

"I think I know where Danko is," I barked into the handheld phone. "He's at Reed College. In Portland. He's a teacher there. Joe, Reed is where Stephen Hardaway went to school. It fits."

Molinari told me he would send an FBI team out to the college while I headed back to the city. I had the lights flashing and the siren on the whole way. South of Vallejo, I couldn't wait any longer. I got the general number for Reed.

I identified myself to an operator and was patched through to the dean of academic studies, a Michael Picotte. FBI agents from the Portland office were arriving as he got on the line.

"We desperately need to locate one of your professors. This is an emergency," I told the dean. "I don't have a name or description. His *real* name is Charles Danko. He'd be approximately fifty years old."

"D-Danko?" Picotte stammered. "There's no one by the name of Danko connected with the college. We have several professors in their fifties, including myself."

I was growing more exasperated and impatient. "Do you have a fax?" I asked. "A fax number I can have?"

I radioed in to the office and got Lorraine on the line. I told her to locate the FBI wanted poster of Charles Danko from the seventies. The resemblance might still be there. Dean Picotte put me on hold as the fax came through.

I was approaching the Bay Bridge; San Francisco International was only about twenty minutes away. I could fly up to Portland myself, I was thinking. Maybe I should get on a plane and go to Reed right now.

"All right, I have it," the dean said, coming back on the line. "This is a wanted poster. . . ."

"Look at it closely," I said. "Please . . . Do you recognize the face?"

"My God . . . ," the dean seemed to choke.

"Who is he? I need a name!" I yelled into the phone. I sensed that Picotte was hesitating. He might be giving up a colleague, even a friend.

I pulled off the bridge into San Francisco and onto Harrison Street. "Dean Picotte, please . . . I need a name! Lives are at stake here."

"Stanzer," the dean finally said. "It looks like Jeffrey Stanzer. I'm almost certain."

I pulled out a pen and hastily scribbled the name down. Jeffrey Stanzer. Stanzer was Danko!

Danko was August Spies. And he was still on the loose.

"Where do we find him?" I said. "There are FBI agents at the college now. We need an address for Stanzer right now."

Picotte hesitated again. "Professor Stanzer's a respected member of our faculty."

I pulled to a halt on the side of the street.

"You have to give us a specific location where we can find Jeffrey Stanzer. This is a homicide investigation! Stanzer is a murderer. He's going to kill again."

The dean exhaled. "You said you were calling from San Francisco?"

"Yes."

There was a pause. "He's down there with you. . . . Jeffrey Stanzer is presenting at the G-8 meeting. I think it's scheduled for tonight."

My God, Danko was going to kill everybody there.

Chapter 102

Charles Danko stood amid the bright lights outside the Palace of the Legion of Honor, and his body jittered with nerves and anticipation. This was *his* night. He was going to be famous, and so would his brother, William.

Anyone who thought they knew him would have been surprised he was speaking in San Francisco tonight. Jeffrey Stanzer had spent years in a secluded academic life, carefully avoiding the public eye. Hiding from the police.

But tonight he was going to do something far bolder than deliver some boring speech.

All the theories and analyses didn't mean anything now. Tonight, he would rewrite history.

Every cop in San Francisco was looking for him, August Spies. And the laugh was, they were letting him in—right through the front door!

A chill cut through him. He clutched his briefcase tightly against his rumpled tuxedo. Inside was his speech, an analysis of the effect of invested foreign capital on the labor markets of the Third World. His life's work, some might say. But what did anyone really know about him? Not a thing. Not even his name.

Up ahead, security agents dressed in tuxedos and gowns were poking through the pockets and purses of economists and ambassadors' wives, the kind of self-important, self-involved functionaries who flocked to this sort of thing.

I could kill all of them, he was thinking. *And why not?* They came to carve up the world, to put their economic thumbprint on those who could not compete, or even fight back. *Bloodsuckers,* he thought. *Ugly, despicable human beings. Everyone here deserves to die. Just like Lightower and Bengosian.*

The line made its way past a cast of Rodin's *The Thinker.* Another flutter of nerves rippled through his limbs. Finally, Danko presented his special VIP invitation to an attractive woman dressed in a black evening dress. Probably FBI. No doubt a Glock was strapped underneath her gown. *Chicks with dicks,* Danko thought.

"Good evening, sir," she said and checked his name against a list. "We apologize for any inconvenience, Professor Stanzer, but can I ask you to place your case through security?"

"Of course. It's just my speech, though," Danko said, handing her his briefcase like any nervous academic. He extended his arms while a security guard waved a metal-detector wand up and down his body.

The security man felt around his jacket. "What's this?" he asked. Danko removed a small plastic canister. There was a pharmaceutical label on it and a prescription made out to him. The canister was another of Stephen Hardaway's masterpieces. Poor dead Stephen. Poor Julia, Robert, and Michelle. Soldiers. *Just like him.*

"For my asthma," Danko said. He coughed a little and pointed to his chest. "Proventil.

Always need it before a speech. I even have a backup."

The guard regarded it for a moment. This was good fun, actually. He and Stephen had perfected the canister. Who needed guns and bombs when all the terror in the world was right in the palm of his hand.

William would be proud!

"You can go inside, sir." The guard finally waved Charles Danko ahead. "Have a good night."

"Oh, I plan to."

Chapter 103

I gunned my Explorer, careening through a red light on Ness heading toward Geary. The Palace of the Legion of Honor was all the way out at Lands End. Even without traffic, I was ten minutes away.

I punched in Molinari's number. His cell phone wasn't accepting.

I tried to get patched through to the Chief. One of his assistants answered and said he was out in the crowd. "The vice president is coming in the room at this very moment," he said. "There he is."

"Listen to me!" I shouted as I swerved, siren blaring, through parting traffic. "I want

you to find Tracchio or Molinari, whomever you see first. Put this phone in their ear. *This is a matter of national emergency.* I don't care who the hell they're talking with! Go! Now!"

My eyes flashed to the clock on my dash. A bomb could go off at any time. All we had was a thirty-year-old likeness to identify Charles Danko. I wasn't sure if I could pick him out myself.

A minute passed very slowly. Then a voice crackled back over my cell phone. Molinari. Finally.

"Joe," I said into the phone, "just listen, please. Charles Danko's there! Right now! He's going by the name Jeffrey Stanzer. He's a speaker at the conference. I'll be there in about three minutes. Take him down, Joe!"

Quickly, we argued the pros and cons of emptying the Palace or making some kind of warning announcement using Stanzer's name. Molinari decided against. The first sign of alarm, he might decide to set off whatever he was planning.

Finally I spun onto Thirty-fourth, into the park, then up the hill to the Legion of Honor.

The park was banded by demonstrators. Barricades blocked the way.

Patrolmen were checking IDs. I lowered the driver's window and held out my shield—pounding the horn as hard as I could.

I was finally able to maneuver through the narrow lane of stretch limos and police cars that led up to the main circle of the Palace. I ditched the Explorer in front of the arced, columned gate. Started to run. I kept bumping into Feds transmitting on radios—flashing my badge. *"Let me through!"*

At last I pushed my way inside the main building. The halls were packed—statesmen, dignitaries.

I spotted Molinari, giving orders into a handheld radio. I rushed up to him. "He's here," he said. "His name's checked off on the guest list. He's already inside."

Chapter 104

There were ambassadors, cabinet members, business leaders everywhere, chatting in crowds, sipping champagne. Any second a bomb could go off. The vice president was being moved to safety. But Charles Danko could be anywhere. What he had in mind, God only knew. We didn't even know what the bastard looked like now!

Molinari handed me a walkie-talkie dialed to his frequency. "I've got the wanted sheet. I'll go left. Keep in touch with me, Lindsay. No heroes tonight." I started to weave through the crowd. In my mind I drew an image of Charles Danko thirty years ago and transposed it onto every face I saw. I wished I'd asked the dean at Reed for some kind of current description. Everything had happened too fast. It still was going too fast.

Where are you, Danko, you son of a bitch?

"I'm searching the main room," I spoke into the walkie-talkie. "I don't see him."

"I'm here in the annex," Molinari replied. "Nothing so far. But he's here."

I was staring intently at every face. Our only advantage was that he didn't know we knew. A few Feds were quietly escorting people toward the exits. We couldn't cause a panic and give ourselves away.

But I didn't see him anywhere. Where was Danko? What was he planning tonight? It had to be big—he was here himself.

"I'm heading in to the Rodins," I told Molinari. There were large, recognizable bronzes on marble pedestals all around me, and people sipping champagne. I came upon a crowd gathered near one of the statues.

"What's going on here?" I asked a woman in a black gown.

"The vice president," she said. "He's scheduled here any moment." The vice president had been whisked away, but no one had been told. These people were milling around for an introduction. Would Danko be here, too?

I scanned the line, face to face.

I saw a tall, thin man, balding on top. He had a high brow. Close, narrow eyes. A hand in his jacket pocket. I felt a cold spot near the center of my chest.

I could see the resemblance to the picture from thirty years ago. There were people milling about, blocking my view. But there was no mistaking it—Charles Danko was the image of his father.

I turned my head away and spoke into my walkie-talkie. "I found him! Joe, he's here."

Danko was in line to meet the vice president. My heart was beating furiously. His left hand was still in his jacket pocket. Was he holding some kind of detonator? How could he get it in here?

"I'm in the room with the Rodins. Joe, I'm looking right at him."

Molinari said, "Stay there. I'm coming. Don't take any chances."

Suddenly Danko's gaze drifted to me. I didn't know if he'd seen me on TV as part of the investigation, or if I had "cop" written on my face. Somehow he seemed to know. Our eyes locked.

I saw him get out of the line he was standing in. He kept his eyes on me.

I took a step toward him. Opened my jacket for my gun. At least a dozen people were blocking my way. I had to get through. I lost sight of Danko for just a second. No more than that.

When the opening cleared again, Danko was no longer there.

The white rabbit was gone again.

Chapter 105

I pushed my way up to where he'd been standing seconds ago. *Gone!* I scanned the room. "I lost him," I spat into the walkie-talkie. "He must've ducked into the crowd. Son of a bitch!" For no good reason, I was mad at myself.

I didn't see Charles Danko anywhere. All the men were wearing tuxedos, looking the same. And all those people were exposed to danger, maybe even death.

I badged my way through a barricade and ran down a long corridor that led to the closed-off section of the museum. Still no sign of Danko. I ran back to the main ballroom and bumped into Molinari.

"He's here. I know he is, Joe. This is his moment."

Molinari nodded and radioed that no one, under any circumstance, was to leave the building. I was thinking that if any kind of device went off in there, with all those people, it would be a total disaster. I'd die, too. And Molinari. It would be worse than the Rincon Center.

Where are you, Danko?

Then I caught a glimpse of him again. I thought so anyway. I pointed toward a tall balding man. He was circling away from us, ducking in and out of the crowd. "That's him!"

"Danko!" I yelled, pulling my Glock from its shoulder holster. "Danko! Stop!"

The crowd parted enough for me to see him remove a hand from his jacket pocket. He caught my eyes again—and then he smiled at me. What the hell did he have?

"Police!" Molinari shouted. "Everybody down!"

Charles Danko's fingers were wrapped around something. I couldn't tell if it was a gun, or maybe a detonator.

Then I saw it—a plastic canister in his hand. What the hell was it? He raised his arm and I charged. There was no other choice.

Seconds later I crashed into Charles Danko, grabbing at his arm, hoping the canister would break free. I latched on to his hand, desperately trying to pry the canister free. I couldn't budge it.

I heard him grunt in pain, saw him twisting the canister toward me. Right at my face.

Molinari was on the other side of Danko, trying to wrestle him down, too. "Get away from him!" I heard him yell at me. The canister turned again—toward Molinari. Everything was happening fast, in just a few seconds.

I held on to Danko's arm. I had some leverage. I was trying to break his arm.

He turned toward me, and our eyes met. I'd never felt such hatred, such coldness. "Bastard!" I yelled in his face. "Remember Jill!"

In that second, I squeezed the canister.

Spray shot into his face. Very close in. Danko coughed, gasped. His face twisted into a horrified mask. Other agents had him now. They pulled him away from me.

Danko was breathing heavily. He was still

coughing, as if he could spit back the poison from his lungs.

"It's over," I gasped. "You're over. You're done. You *lost*, asshole."

His eyes smiled vacantly. He motioned me closer. "It will never be over, you fool. There's always another soldier."

That's when I heard shots, and understood that I *was* a fool.

Chapter 106

We rushed out to the courtyard, where the shots had come from. Joe Molinari and I pushed our way through the crowd. People were gasping, a few had started to weep.

I couldn't see what had happened, and then I could. And I wished that I hadn't.

Eldridge Neal was on his back, a crimson stain widening across his white shirt. Someone had shot the vice president of the United States. My God, not another American tragedy like this.

A woman was being held down by Secret Service agents; she couldn't have been much older than eighteen or nineteen. Frizzy red hair. She was screaming at the vice president, rambling on about babies being sold into slavery in the Sudan; AIDS killing millions in Africa; corporate war crimes in Iraq and Syria. She must have been waiting for Neal as he was moved out of the main hall.

Suddenly I recognized the girl. I'd seen her before, in Roger Lemouz's office. The girl who'd given me the finger when I told her to leave. Hell, she was just a kid.

Joe Molinari let go of my arm and went to the aid of the vice president. The cursing, screaming girl was pulled away. Meanwhile, an ambulance drove right into the courtyard. EMS medics jumped out and began to tend to Vice President Neal.

Had Charles Danko planned this?

Had he known we were on to him?

Was this a setup? Knowing that chaos would reign if we caught up with him? What had he said? There's always another soldier.

That was the scariest thing of all. I knew that Danko was right.

Chapter 107

I was supposed to go to the hospital to be examined, but I wouldn't do it. Not yet. Joe Molinari and I went with the red-haired girl back to the Hall. We interrogated Annette Breiling for several hours, and then this revolutionary, this terrorist, this person who could shoot the vice president in cold blood, she cracked.

Annette Breiling told us everything we needed to know, and more, about the plot at the Palace of the Legion of Honor.

It was four in the morning when we arrived in an upscale neighborhood in Kensington, a couple of towns over from Berkeley. There were at least half a dozen patrol cars there and everybody was heavily armed. The street was in the hills and had a view of the San Pablo Reservoir. Very pretty, surprisingly posh. It didn't look as if anything bad could happen here.

"He lives well," said Molinari, but that was it for small talk. "Let's you and I do the honors."

The front door was opened by the Lance Hart Professor of Romance Languages, Roger Lemouz. He had on a terry-cloth robe, and his curly black hair was in disarray. His eyes were glassy and red, and I wondered if he had been drinking that night, if Lemouz had been celebrating.

"Madam Inspector," he said in a throaty whisper, "you're beginning to wear out your welcome. It's four A.M. This is my home."

I didn't bother to exchange unpleasantries with Lemouz, and neither did Molinari. "You're under arrest for conspiracy to commit murder," he said, then pushed his way inside.

Lemouz's wife and two children appeared, entering the living room behind him, which was unfortunate. The boy was no more than twelve, the girl even younger. Molinari and I holstered our guns.

"Charles Danko is dead," I told Lemouz. "A

young woman you know named Annette Breiling has implicated you in the murder of Jill Bernhardt, all of the murders, Lemouz. She told us that you were the one who set up Stephen Hardaway's cell. You delivered Julia Marr and Robert Green into the cell. And you controlled Charles Danko—you knew how to push his buttons. His anger seethed for thirty years, but you got Danko to act on it. He was your puppet."

Lemouz laughed in my face. "I don't know any of these people. Well, Ms. Breiling was a student of mine. She dropped out of the university, however. This is a huge mistake and I'm calling my lawyer right now if you don't leave."

"You're under arrest," Joe Molinari said, making the obvious official. "Want to hear your rights, Professor? I want to read them to you."

Lemouz smiled, and it was strange and eerie. "You still don't understand, do you? Neither of you. This is why you are doomed. One day your entire country will crumble. It's already happening."

"Why don't you explain what we're missing?" I spat the words at him.

He nodded, then Lemouz turned toward his family. "You're missing this." His small son was holding a handgun, and it was obvious that he knew how to use it. The boy's eyes were as cold as his father's.

"I'll kill you both," he said. "It would be my pleasure."

"The army that is building against you is massive, their cause is just. Women, children, so many soldiers, Madam Inspector. Think about it. The Third World War—it's begun."

Lemouz walked calmly to his family and took the gun from his son. He kept it aimed at us. Then he kissed his wife, his daughter, his son. The kisses were tender and heartfelt. Tears were in his wife's eyes. Lemouz whispered something to each of them.

He backed out of the living room; then we could hear running footsteps. A door slammed somewhere in the house. How could he hope to get away?

A gunshot sounded loudly inside the house.

Molinari and I ran in that direction.

We found him in the bedroom—he'd killed himself, shot one bullet into his right temple.

His wife and children had begun to wail in the other room.

So many soldiers, I was thinking. *This won't stop, will it? This Third World War.*

Chapter 108

Charles Danko didn't spray me with ricin. That was what the doctors were saying, hovering over me all morning at the toxicology unit at Moffit.

And the vice president wasn't going to die. Word was that they had him two floors below me, that he had even been on the phone to his boss in Washington.

I spent several hours with a maze of tubes and wires sticking out of me, monitors reading my blood and chest scans. The contents of Danko's canister were identified as ricin. Enough to kill hundreds of people if he had gone undetected. Danko had ricin in his lungs, and he was going to die. I wasn't sorry to hear it.

About noon I got a phone call from the president, as in *the* president. They stuck a phone to my ear, and in my daze I remembered hearing the word *hero* about six times. The president even said he was looking forward to thanking me in person. I joked that maybe we should wait for the toxic glow to settle down.

When I opened my eyes after a snooze, Joe Molinari was sitting on the corner of my bed.

He smiled. "Hey. I thought I said 'no heroes!'"

I blinked and smiled, too, a little more groggy than triumphant, embarrassed at the tubes and monitors.

"The good news," he said with a wink, "is the doctors say you're fine. They're just holding you for observation a few more hours. There's an armada of press waiting for you out there."

"The bad news?" I said, hoarsely.

"Someone's gonna have to teach you how to dress for these photo ops."

"New fashion look." I squeezed back a smile.

I noticed that he had a raincoat draped over his arm and was wearing the navy herringbone suit I'd seen him in the first time. It was a *very* nice suit, and he wore it well.

"The vice president's recuperating. I'm heading back to Washington tonight."

All I could do was nod. "Okay . . ."

"No"—he shook his head, inching closer—"it's not okay. Because it's not what I want."

"We both knew this would happen," I said, trying to be strong. "You have a job. The interns . . ."

Molinari scowled. "You're brave enough to go after a man holding a canister of deadly poison, but you're not ready to stand up for something you want."

I felt a tear creep out of the corner of my eye. "I don't know what I want, right now."

Molinari put down his raincoat, then drew close and put a hand to my cheek, brushing away the tear. "I think you need some time. You have to decide, when things calm down, if you're prepared to let someone in. Like a relationship, Lindsay."

He took my hand. "My name's *Joe,* Lindsay. Not Molinari, or Deputy Director, wink, wink. And what I'm talking about is you and me. And not trying to joke it away because you've been hurt before. Or because you lost a really close friend. I know this'll come as a disappointment, Lindsay, but you're entitled to be happy. You know what I mean. Call me old-fashioned." He smiled.

"Old-fashioned," I said, doing exactly what he accused me of, making jokes when I ought to be serious.

Something was stuck inside me, the way it always seemed to stick when I wanted to say what was in my heart. "So, you get out here how often?"

"Speeches, security conferences . . . a couple of national crises factored in . . ."

I laughed. "We can't help the jokes, neither of us."

Molinari sighed. "Even you must know this by now: I'm not one of the assholes, Lindsay. It can work. The next step is yours. You have to make a move to try."

He stood up and brushed his hand over my hair. "The doctors assured me that this is perfectly safe." He smiled, then leaned over and planted a kiss on my lips. His lips were soft, and mine, chapped and dry from the night, clung on. I was trying to *show* him how I felt, knowing I'd be crazy not to *tell* him and let him walk out that door.

Joe Molinari stood and draped the raincoat over his arm. "It's been a privilege and an honor getting to know you, Lieutenant Boxer."

"Joe," I said, a little scared to see him go.

"You know where to reach me."

I watched him head to the door. "You never know when a girl might have a national emergency. . . ."

"Yeah"—he turned and smiled—"I'm a national emergency kind of guy."

Chapter 109

Later that afternoon, my doctor came in and told me there was nothing wrong with my system that a good glass of wine or two wouldn't cure.

"There are even some people here who want to take you home," he said.

Outside my room, I saw Claire and Cindy peeking in.

They took me home about long enough to shower, change, and give Martha a long-overdue hug. Then I had to go down to the Hall. Everyone seemed to want a piece of me. I made a date to see the girls later at

Susie's. It was important that we get together now.

I did the news spots on the steps of the Hall. Tom Brokaw was patched through and interviewed me on a video link.

As I recounted the story of how we had found Danko and Hardaway, I felt a tremor snaking through me, distancing me even as I spoke. Jill was dead; Molinari was gone; I didn't feel much like a hero. The phone was going to ring, some other homicide called in, and life would slam back the way it always did. But this time I knew nothing was ever going to be the same.

It was about four-thirty when the girls came to get me. I was doing reports. Although Jacobi and Cappy were bragging they had the best LT on the force, I'd actually felt depressed. Lonely and empty. Until the girls showed up, anyway.

"Hey," Cindy said, twirling a little Mexican cocktail flag in my face, "margaritas await."

They took me to Susie's, the last place we had been with Jill. Actually, two years before, it was where we had welcomed her into our budding group. We took our places in our corner booth and ordered a round of margaritas. I ran them through the terrifying struggle at the Palace the night before, the president's call, then today, Brokaw and the evening news.

It was sad, though, just the three of us. The conspicuous empty space next to Claire.

Our drinks came. "On the house, of course," the waitress, Joanie, said.

We raised our glasses, each of us trying to smile, but fighting back tears. "Here's to our girl," Claire said. "Maybe now she can start to rest in peace."

"She'll never rest in peace," Cindy said, laughing through tears. "Out of character."

"I'm sure she's up there now," I said, "sizing up the pecking order, looking down at us. 'Hey, guys, I got it all figured out. . . .'"

"Then she's smiling," Claire said.

"To Jill," we all said. We clinked glasses. It was hard to think that this was the way it was going to be from now on. I missed her so much, and never more than that moment at our table, without her.

"So," Claire said, clearing her throat, her gaze landing on me. "What happens now?"

"We're gonna order some ribs," I said, "and I'm gonna have another one of these. Maybe more than one."

"I think she was actually saying, what's with you and Deputy Dawg." Cindy winked.

"He's heading back to Washington," I said. "Tonight."

"For good?" Claire asked, surprised.

"That's where the listening devices and sleek black helicopters are." I stirred my drink. "Bell helicopter, I believe."

"Oh." Claire nodded. She glanced toward Cindy. "You *like* this guy, don't you, Lindsay?"

"I like him," I said. I flagged Joanie, ordered another round of drinks.

"I don't mean *like* him, honey. I mean you *really* like him."

"Whad'ya want me to do, Claire? Break out in a chorus of 'Don't he make my brown eyes blue'?"

"No," Claire said, glancing at Cindy, then back to me, "what we want you to do, Lindsay, is put aside whatever it is that's getting in the way of you doing the right thing for yourself, before you let that guy get on his plane."

I arched my back against the booth. I swallowed uneasily. "It's Jill. . . ."

"Jill?"

I took a breath, a sharp rush of tears biting at my eyes. "I wasn't there for her, Claire. The night she threw Steve out."

"What're you talking about?" Claire said. "You were up in Portland."

"I was with Molinari," I said. "When I got back it was after one. Jill sounded mixed up. I said I'd come over, but I didn't press it. You know why? Because I was all dreamy-eyed over Joe. She had just thrown Steve out."

"She said she was okay," Cindy said. "You told us."

"And that was Jill, right? You ever heard her ask for help? Bottom line, I wasn't there for her. And whether it's right or wrong, I can't look at Joe now without seeing her, hearing her needing me, thinking if I had, maybe she'd still be here."

Neither of them said anything. Not a word. I sat there, my jaw tight, pressing back tears.

"I'll tell you what I think," Claire said, her fingers creeping across the table and taking ahold of my hand. "I think you're way too smart, honey, to really think that your enjoying yourself for once in your life made any difference in what happened to Jill. You know she'd be the first one who'd want you to be happy, too."

"I know that, Claire." I nodded. "I just can't put it away. . . ."

"Well, you better put it away," Claire said,

squeezing my hand, "'cause all it is, is you just trying to hurt yourself. Everyone's entitled to be happy, Lindsay. *Even you.*"

I dabbed at a tear with the cocktail napkin. "I already heard that once today," I said, and couldn't hold back a smile.

"Yeah, well, here's to Lindsay Boxer," Claire announced, and raised her glass. "And here's to hoping that for once in her life she hears it loud and clear."

A shout interrupted us from the bar area. Everyone was pointing to the TV. Instead of some dumb ball game, there was my face on the screen. Tom Brokaw was asking me questions. Whistles and cheering broke out.

There I was on the evening news.

Chapter 110

Joe Molinari took a sip of the vodka the flight attendant had brought him, then eased back in his seat aboard the government jet. With any luck he'd sleep all the way to Washington. He hoped so. No, he'd sleep for sure, soundly. For the first time in days.

He'd be fresh to make a report in front of the director of homeland security in the morning. This one was put to bed, he could definitively say. Eldridge Neal would heal. There were reports to write. There might be a congressional subcommittee to go before. There was an anger out there they'd have to keep an eye on. This time the terror hadn't come from abroad.

Molinari leaned back in the plush seat. The scope of the whole remarkable chain of events was becoming clear in his eyes. From the moment that Sunday he was informed of the bombing in San Francisco to taking out Danko as he wrestled with Lindsay Boxer at the G-8 reception last night. He knew what to write: the names and details, the sequence of events, the outcome. He knew how to explain everything, he thought. Except one thing.

Her. Molinari shut his eyes and felt incredibly melancholy.

How to explain the electricity shooting through him every time their arms brushed. Or the feeling he got when he looked into Lindsay's deep green eyes. She was so hard and tough — and so gentle and vulnerable. A lot like him. And she was funny, too, when she wanted to be anyway, which was often.

He wished he could do the big romantic thing, like in the movies, whisk her on a plane and take her somewhere. Call in to the office: *That subcommittee meeting will have to wait, sir.* Molinari felt a smile creep over his face.

"Takeoff should be in about five, sir," the flight attendant informed him.

"Thank you," he said, nodding. *Try to relax. Chill. Sleep.* He willed himself, thought of home. He'd been living out of a suitcase for two weeks now. It may not be how he wanted this to end, but it would be good to be home. He closed his eyes once more.

"Sir," the attendant called again. A uniformed airport policeman had boarded the plane. He was escorted back to him.

"I'm sorry, sir," the policeman said. "Something urgent has come up. I was told to hold the plane at the gate and accompany you back inside. The police gave me this number for you to call."

A stab of worry jolted Molinari. What the hell could have happened now? He took the piece of paper and grabbed his briefcase and phone. He punched in the number, told the pilot to wait, and followed the security man off the plane. He put the phone to his ear.

Chapter 111

My phone started to ring just as Molinari appeared near the gate. I stood there and watched him. Seeing me, the phone to my ear, he began to understand. A smile came over his face, a *big* smile.

I'd never been so nervous in my life. Then we just stood there, maybe fifteen feet apart. He'd stopped walking.

"I'm the emergency," I said into the phone. "I need your help."

At first Molinari smiled, then he caught himself, with that stern deputy director sort of look. "You're lucky. I'm an emergency kind of guy."

"I have no life," I said. "I have this very nice dog. And my friends. And this job. And I'm good at it. But I have no life."

"And what is it you want?" Molinari said, stepping closer.

His eyes were twinkling and forgiving. They reflected some kind of joy—cutting through the case, and the continent that divided us—the same thing that was in my heart.

"You," I said. "I want you. *And* the jet."

He laughed, and then he stood right in front of me.

"No"—I shook my head—"I just want *you*. I couldn't let you get on that plane without telling you that. This bicoastal thing, we can try to make it work if you like. You say you're out here every once in a while for conferences and the occasional national crisis. . . . *Me,* I get back there now and then. I got an invitation to stay at the White House recently. You've been to the White House, Joe. We can—"

"Sshhh." He put a finger to my lips. Then he bent and kissed me right there in the skyway. I was so caught up in trying to be open for once, I swallowed my own words. My spine went rigid, and God, it felt so natural, so right for him to be holding me. I wrapped my fingers around his arms, holding on as tightly as I could.

When we let go, Molinari curled a grin at me. "So, you got an invitation to the White House, huh? I always wondered what it'd be like to sleep in the Lincoln Bedroom."

"Keep dreaming." I laughed into those blue eyes of his. Then I locked my arm around his and led him back toward the terminal. "Now your desk at the Capitol, Mr. Deputy Director. *That* sounds a bit more interesting. . . ."

About the Author

James Patterson's most recent major international bestseller is *The Lake House*. He is the author of twenty-four books and lives in Florida.